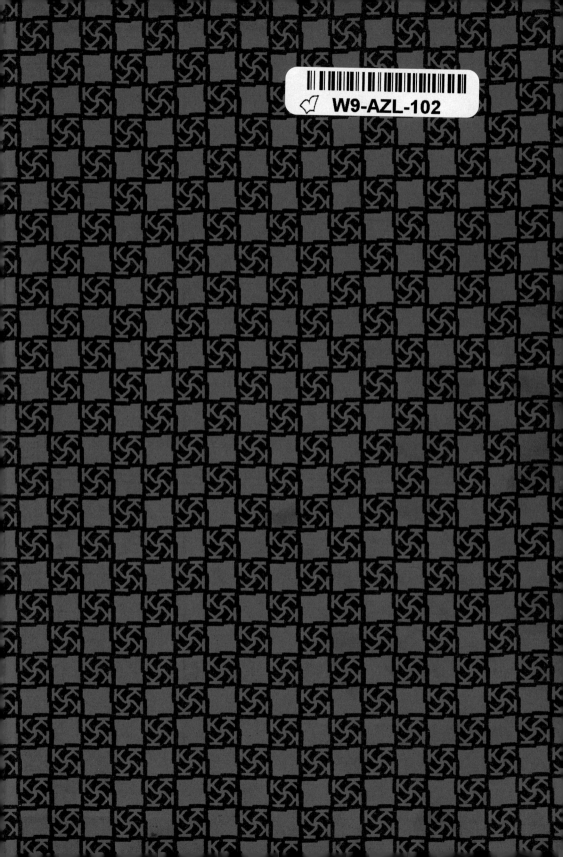

W9-AZL-102

Cinema at the Bio Lucerna Prague, c. 1914

Hanni Weisse silent film star

Kiosk advertising cultural events Paris, 1910

Still from *The Other* featuring Albert Bassermann 1913

Omnia Pathé Cinémathèque Paris, 1907

Still from *The Other* 1913

Movie posters on the Piazza d'Erbe Verona, 1913

Franz Kafka c. 1906

Kafka Goes to the Movies

HANNS ZISCHLER

Translated by Susan H. Gillespie

A Winterhouse Book

THE UNIVERSITY OF CHICAGO PRESS

CHICAGO & LONDON

Hanns Zischler, born in 1947 in Nuremburg, is an an actor and publicist.
He has directed TV movies and live theater and has appeared in films
by Chabrol, Godard, and Wim Wenders. He is a cofounder of Merve and
Alpheus Publishers. His most recent publications are *Day Trips* (1993)
and *You Can't Judge a Book by Its Cover* (1995). He has lived in Berlin
since 1968.

Susan H. Gillespie is the director of the Institute for International
Liberal Education at Bard College and translator of works by Theodor
Adorno, Friedrich Hölderlin, and Helga Königsdorf, among others.

The University of Chicago Press, Chicago 60637
The University of Chicago Press, Ltd., London
© 2003 by The University of Chicago

Designed by Winterhouse Studio
Falls Village, Connecticut 06031

All rights reserved. Published 2003
Printed in China
12 11 10 09 08 07 06 05 04 03   1 2 3 4 5
ISBN 0-226-98671-3 (cloth)

Originally published as *Kafka geht ins Kino,* © 1996 Rowohlt Verlag GmbH.

Library of Congress Cataloging-in-Publication Data
Zischler, Hanns, 1947–
    [Kafka geht ins Kino. English]
    Kafka goes to the movies / Hanns Zischler ; translated by Susan H. Gillespie.
        p. cm.
Includes index.
    ISBN 0-226-98671-3 (alk. paper)
    1. Kafka, Franz, 1883–1924 — Knowledge — Motion pictures.
2. Silent films — History. I. Title
    PT2621.A26 Z37 2002
    833'.912 — dc21

♾ The paper used in this publication meets the minimum
requirements of the American National Standard for Information Sciences —
Permanence of Paper for Printed Library Materials, ANSI Z39.48–1992.

für Regina

CONTENTS

KAFKA GOES TO THE MOVIES

Still from *The White Slave Girl* 1911

PREFACE

*Because in the cinematograph — this is its infinite value
and advantage compared with the stage —
all bothersome reality appears as if wiped away.*

Alfred Polgar, 1912

I was working on a television movie about Kafka in 1978 when I first
came across the notes on the cinema in his early diaries and letters. The
notes were very scattered, occasionally curt and cryptic. Despite their
sporadic character, the excited, passionate, and at times melancholy
tone suggested strong feelings associated with Kafka's experience of
moviegoing. Oddly, these comments came to an almost complete stop
toward the end of 1913.

Once I started to take a deeper interest in the topic, I was surprised
by the strange lack of concern shown by scholars. It was evidently the
dubious source value of the cinema that prevented literary scholars
from even attempting a more detailed investigation. At first glance, the
course the research would have to follow did not seem terribly complicated to me. One would simply have to compare Kafka's own notes,
which were sparse but as precise as a bookkeeper's, with the advertisements in the daily press in order to identify the films themselves. Since a
number of visits to the cinema had occurred during Kafka's bachelor
trips with Max Brod, it seemed natural to revisit certain places —
Munich, Milan, Paris. But over the years the research turned out to be
quite a complex undertaking.

What had begun out of sheer curiosity gradually developed into regular detective work, spurred on by the images and texts that were

Still from *Shivat Zion* (Return to Zion), discussed in the chapter "Afternoon, Palestine Film."

emerging from archives and private collections. In 1983, I was able to publish preliminary findings in *Freibeuter*, and a few years later I published additional discoveries in the Swiss yearbook *Cinema* and the French journal *Trafic*.

For the most part, I was carrying out this research in the shadow of my work as a movie actor, as often as opportunities arose. This period, which continued for a long time, brought me into direct and epistolary contact with people whose archival memory opened up only gradually, over the course of extended time periods and repeated encounters.

The more material I was able to find, the more difficult it became to prove that certain films were actually no longer extant. The late Swiss film historian Fritz Güttinger, who assisted me in every conceivable way, had an ironic-fatalistic expression for this phenomenon: "film gap history."

The rediscovery of the Zionist film *Shivat Zion* is a vivid example of this particular kind of evidentiary conundrum. After an initial, false start, following a vague hunch, I went looking for the film in the Prague Film

Archives. Under the regime of bureaucratic socialism, the search for a Zionist film was a rather dicey business. Besides, my status as an unaffiliated researcher was not exactly made to order for gaining ready access to the jealously guarded archives. Numerous letters of reference graciously provided by Enno Patalas from the Munich Museum of Cinematography and Eva Orbanz and Hans-Helmuth Prinzler of the Stiftung Deutsche Kinemathek gradually eased my way into the Prague sources. In the end, it was Ždenek Štábl, the late historian of Prague silent films, who in 1987—after I had repeatedly shown him all the descriptions of this film that I had collected—suddenly and "promptly," as he put it, recalled certain images and shots. "I know this film," he told me. "It is in the film archive here. I never until this moment knew that it is called *Shivat Zion*." Even then, it would be some time before I would be able to view the—extremely well-restored—print myself.

In the winter of 1984, in Verona, I had been searching long and unsuccessfully for an illustration of the long-vanished Cinema Calzoni. It was probably at this cinema that in 1913 Kafka had seen a film that moved him to tears. I can no longer say which friendly denizen of Verona pointed me one December evening in the direction of Pino Breanza, a baker who has his stand on the Piazza d'Erbe and is a highly respected local historian. No sooner had Signore Breanza heard my request than he rushed home, abandoning his stand, soon to return and, beaming, hand me an original photograph of the cinema in question. Another time it was the estimable former chief of restoration of the Cinémathèque Française, Vincent Pinel, who helped me locate a source that I had believed lost. Long after I had given up hope of ever finding even a single image from *La Broyeuse de Coeurs*, whose ghost haunts one of Kafka's letters to Felice, Pinel led me into the witches' cauldron of the cinémathèque, the restoration laboratory, where two women in huge rubber gloves fished a few rolls of film out of a veritable snakes' nest of negatives and held them up to the light, and the "heartbreaker" appeared to me in all her translucent beauty.

Not until all the photographs, programs, program notes, and advertisements were laid out in front of me like an arbitrarily assembled photo album could I even think about decoding the text. By Kafka's "text" I mean the diaries and letters, above all the letters to Felice, and not the fiction. Kafka's comments on the cinema, as compiled by Gustav Janouch, were of no value for my inquiry.

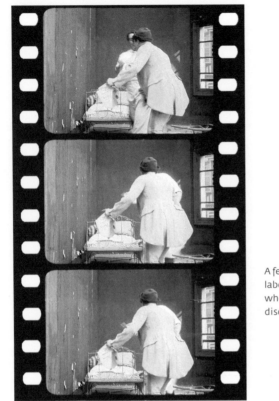

A few frames of discarded footage from the laboratory of the Cinémathèque Française, where Vincent Pinel restored *The Heartbreaker*, discussed on PP. 77–81.

Franz Kafka plays the moviegoer in a bachelor theater that he directed again and again, with melancholy wit, in the company of Max Brod and other Prague friends, until 1912–13. The images that were scattered across the years, and are recollected here, are the stage sets among which we can identify the portrait of Franz Kafka as moviegoer. It is certainly no accident that Kafka's most extensive remarks on the subject of movies and moviegoing are found in his late-night letters to Felice Bauer. She is his privileged audience; for her he projects his sleepwalking adventures onto the giant screen of his correspondence.

Naturally, my research was not free of assumptions. It draws on the results of the biographical research on Kafka, above all on the great, pathbreaking work of Klaus Wagenbach and Hartmut Binder, and not least on the critical edition of Kafka's works.

For numerous tips, encouraging words, and assistance both practical and theoretical, I am indebted, in addition to those individuals mentioned above, to Bettina Augustin, Werner Birett, Henryk Broder, Karel Černy, Marguerite Engberg, Jeannine Fiedler, Maria Gazzetti, Michael Glasmeier, Marlis Gerhardt, Nurdan Kling, Annelen Kranefuss, Jean Lemagny, Vladimir Opelka of Filmnovy Ustav Prag, Sir Malcolm Pasley, Christa Schabaz, Pavel Scheufler, the Stiftung Deutsche Kinemathek Berlin, and Herr Ullmann of the Munich Museum of Cinematography. Special thanks are due to my friend Hans-Gerd Koch of the Kafka Forschungsstelle Wuppertal, who helped me out time and again with his "briefings." I am grateful for the patience, hard work, and sense of proportion of the Rowohlt Verlag in the persons of Delf Schmidt, Andreas Anter, and Joachim Düster.

The Arrival of a Train at the Station of La Ciotat Lumière brothers, 1895

THE AUDIENCE

*I thank you sincerely, my dear Max, except that the unclarity of the facts is still more
clear to me than your explanation. The only thing I can say with any conviction about all this
is that we will have to pay more lengthy and numerous visits to the cinema,
the factory floor, and the geishas before we can understand this matter
not only for ourselves but for the world.*

Kafka, letter to Max Brod, August 22, 1908

4

"The onlookers freeze when the train goes by." We don't know what inci-
dent it was that caused Franz Kafka to open his *Arbeitsheft* with this
sentence. The stupor and the shock—closely tied to the history of the
railroad—that are recorded in this sentence are preserved more than
once in early cinematic history. This first sentence, which leaps out at the
reader in the eternal present of an experiment, oscillates between the
onlookers and the train on the screen. A jump, a quick pan. A montage of
the "here" of the onlookers and the "there" of the train, something that is
all the more startling because Kafka gives no explanation beyond the sentence itself. No opening credits, transition, or ending deliver the reader
from his fright. The shock of the moving picture (both moving past and
moving in itself) gives Kafka cause to reflect. The next sentence, separated from the first by a dash—"'As often as he asks me' the sound of the long
'e' detached from the sentence flew away like a ball over the field"—varies
and transposes the paradox of perception from the cinematographic to
the graphic plane.

Kafka's journal entry sounds like a distant echo, a protoliterary reminiscence of the first milliseconds of the cinematic big bang. Already, it
reveals the problem that, from now on, confronts the moviegoer and
diary-keeper: What can be experienced during the assault of the images,
and how can it be preserved? This is a problem for the increasingly shat-

5

6

tered faculties of perception less in a physical than in a literary sense. The entire spectrum of little trances of the moviegoer, the tears, the distraction, the boundless entertainment, are the affective traces and echoes of images that Kafka has conveyed only very sporadically in the sense of an actual description of scenes in his writing.

Hesitantly but quite self-consciously, the recently graduated Dr. Juris Kafka begins to understand himself as a writer. In 1908 and 1909, comments on and further elaborations of his reading still compete with his own fiction. In the journal *Hyperion*, edited by Franz Blei and Carl Sternheim, he publishes, still anonymously, a series of little prose texts. In October 1907, he lands his first job—as an assistant at the insurance company Assicurazioni Generali. In August 1908, he is offered a position—under slightly better conditions—with the Workers' Accident Insurance Company for the Kingdom of Bohemia in Prague. He is punctilious in his work but dreadfully bored. He divides his free time between his responsibilities to the business that is run by his strict father, various escapades (coffeehouse, cinema, cabaret, bordello) with a growing circle of friends, and his attempts at writing, which gradually assume a more decisive shape. This is the beginning of "Wedding Preparations in the Country" and, soon after, "Description of a Struggle." Spurred on by his reading of Rudolf Kassner's essay "Diderot," Kafka drafts a literary trompe l'œil, a playfully grotesque capriccio in whose turbulence everyday sensory data disappear as completely as if they were mere kinetic shadow play and slapstick despair: **Lately already I wrote the following sentence relating to Kassner and a few other things: "There are things never seen, heard or even felt by us that cannot be proven, either, though no one has yet made the attempt, that we nevertheless immediately chase after, even though we can't tell what direction they are going in, that we overtake before we have caught up with them, and that we then fall into with all our clothes, family keepsakes, and social relations as if into a ditch that was nothing but a shadow on the path.**

From now on, Max Brod, to whom these lines are addressed, becomes Kafka's preferred conversation partner. Toward the end of 1908, Kafka writes to Elsa Taussig—the future Frau Brod—a curious, whimsical letter that reveals a good deal about his mood at the time and about the pleasure he is taking in the primitive movies. In it he expresses an urgent movie recommendation, which, as he writes, grows into a positively principled consideration of the "superfluous" and the "necessary." The

Grand-Kinematograph

„ORIENT"

Hibernergasse Nr. 20
(vis - a - vis Staatsbahnhof.)
Grösstes und vornehmstes Kinematograph-
Theater Prags.
Eigenes Künstler-Orchester 34448
vom 25-31. Dezember.

Grosses Weihnachts-Festprogramm.

u. a.: Ludwig XVII. histor. Drama.
Bahnbau in Afrika etc.
Beginn der Vorstellungen an den Feiertagen:
Nchm. 2, 4, 6 Uhr., und Abd. 8 Uhr.
Vorstellungsdauer ca. 2 Stunden.

The Grand-Kinematograph Orient opened on October 18, 1907. Its proprietors were the Oeser brothers. At first, it went by the name Electric Theater, but from May 1908 on it was known as the Orient. It was the second cinema in Prague to have a permanent home. The poster above calls it the "largest and most distinguished cinematograph theater in Prague." Among the amusing scenes that are announced for the "big Christmas celebration program" are those that Kafka recommended. From the documentary *Bahnbau in Afrika (Railroad Building in Africa)*.

content, the occasion for the letter, is as straightforward as it is complex from an epistolary point of view—evidently Elsa Taussig has asked Kafka to give her a sample of his handwriting. After having been unable or unwilling to respond immediately, Kafka apologizes in writing and at length for the omission. In the process, he provides the desired handwriting sample and does not tire of reminding the fräulein about a plan to go to see two short films at the Kinematographen Theater:

Dear Fräulein,

Do not be alarmed, I only wish to remind you, as agreed and in good time (and as late as possible, so you don't forget about it) that you and your sister wanted to go to the Orient this evening.

If I write more, it is superfluous and even diminishes the significance of the above, but it has always been easier for me to do what is superfluous than what is almost necessary. This almost necessary is something to which I have always given short shrift, I confess. I can confess it because it is natural.

For we are so happy to have done the things that are absolutely

Pathé frères. Kinematographen und Films, Berlin W. 8
Friedrichstr. 191. Eingang Kronenstr. 14.

2. Serie.

Komische Szenen.

2547

Telegr.-Code: *Football.*

Der durstige Gendarm.

Länge 100 m.   Preis Mk. 100.—

Der Gendarm Gérome steht vor der Tür eines Cabarets und schaut nach dem Matrosen Guyot aus, welcher das Schiff verlassen hat und nicht wieder zurückgekehrt ist. Es dauert auch nicht lange so schwankt der Matrose, wie ein Schiff im Sturm, zur Tür heraus und der Gendarm ergreift ihn ohne Schwierigkeit. Aber nach einigen Schritten entweicht der Matrose durch die Beine des Schutzmanns und versteckt sich in den Kasten eines kleinen Geschäftsrades. Gérome eilt hinzu, schliesst den Deckel und setzt sich, der Sicherheit halber, oben auf den Deckel, während der Inhaber des Wagen losradelt.

Doch der Gendarm und der Führer des Rades bekommen in der Hitze Durst und machen in einem Restaurant halt und so fort, bis beide viel betrunkener sind, als der Matrose. Dieser benutzt dann auch einen günstigen Augenblick zu entkommen und der Schutzmann kommt ohne Beute zur Wache, total betrunken.

This film notice summarizes the plot of *The Thirsty Gendarme*, from Pathé Frères Cinematographs and Films, as follows:

The gendarme Jerome stands outside the door of a cabaret keeping an eye out for the sailor Guyot, who has left the ship and failed to return. Not long afterward, the sailor lurches through the door like a ship in a storm, and the gendarme apprehends him without difficulty. But after a few steps, the sailor escapes between the legs of his guard and hides in the box of a small delivery cycle. Jerome hurries after him, shuts the lid, and sits down, for security's sake, on top of it, as the cycle's owner rides off with both of them in tow.

But the gendarme and the cyclist become thirsty in the heat and stop at a tavern, and so forth, until they are both much drunker than the sailor. The latter seizes a favorable opportunity to escape, and the policeman arrives at the station without his prey, utterly drunk.

—TRANS.

The cinema is the ideal of a popular play, or perhaps it is the dramatic ideal itself, for a film sees everything as motion and events; there is not the slightest crack where anything epic or lyrical could take root. And yet the film does not give us soulless circus acts. There are souls concealed within its moving bodies. The viewer must guess at them, he himself must write the text for the images, and this process, as his imagination is drawn in and forced to become a part of their creation, explains the passionate involvement of the moviegoer. This is precisely where the explanation for the interest of the cultivated public is to be found. And finally, the cinema, as democratic as it is, offers educated viewers an advantage in comparison to more simple-minded people. The latter see the images that roll by in unbroken illusion as real, physical life; the educated person knows that he has to do with shadows and takes pleasure in this. Victor Klemperer, "Das Kino im Urtetil bekannter Zeitgenossen" (The Cinema in the Opinion of Well-known Contemporaries), in *Der Kinematograph* (September 25, 1912). The editors present Victor Klemperer with the words, "A pugnacious young literary figure who writes with the rare courage to express his opinion even when it comes to the authorities."

necessary (obviously they have to happen right away, or else how could we keep ourselves alive for the cinematograph—don't forget about this evening—for doing calisthenics and ink drawings, for having our own apartment, for good apples, for sleep when we have already slept our fill, for being drunk, for this or that from the past, for a hot bath in wintertime, when it is already dark, and for who knows what else), we are so happy about this, I assert, that because we are so happy we then do what is almost superfluous but fail to do precisely what is almost necessary.

I mention this only because after that evening at your apartment I knew that it was almost necessary for me to write to you. I completely neglected to do this, that much is certain, because after the most recent show at the cinematograph—you must not get these things confused—the letter in question was still almost necessary, and yet this incidental sort of necessity already lay somewhat in the past, but naturally in a different and formally less valued direction than the one in which the superfluous is to be found.

Lately, when you said I should write to you in order to give a sample of my handwriting, you immediately provided me with all the prerequisites for the necessary and, hence, for the superfluous.

And yet that almost necessary letter would not have been bad. You must consider that what is necessary always occurs, and what is superfluous usually, but what is almost necessary, at least in my case, rarely, as a result of which, robbed of all context, it can become slightly pathetic, i.e., amusing.

So it is a shame about that letter, for it is a shame about your laughter over that letter, by which—surely you believe me—I don't mean to say anything against your other laughter, nor, for example, about the laughter that *The Gallant Guardsman*, or indeed *The Thirsty Gendarme*, will cause you this evening.

Your Franz K.

9

10

13

Poster for an Italian film distributor in *Filma* Milan, September 1908

THE EXPLAINER

The eye experiences sensual pleasure like the ear,
and writing, which is then a matter for the rationally thinking mind,
becomes separated from the work of the nerves.

Rudolf Borchardt, 1898

11

The widespread ambulatory film showings that took place in Prague beginning in 1896 were joined in 1907 by the first permanent cinema, located in the house known as the Blue Pike (U Modré Štiky) located at Karlsgasse 180. It was run by Viktor Ponrepo, who together with his brother advertised the performances on fanciful postcards. They promised their visitors "scenes from life and the world of dreams" that were capable of nothing less than "satisfying all the spectator's needs." What made this movie house memorable for the residents of Prague was, above all, the fact that the two Ponrepos put on magic shows between film showings and accompanied the films as practiced "explainers" or "reciters." The Ponrepos were participants in the action that was shown on the screen. The Yiddish term for them is *Versteller*—a word that plays on both the German *verstellen*, to distort or disguise, and *vorstellen*, to imagine or present.

The film journalist Ulrich Rauscher recorded the performance of one such "explainer" in 1912 in Berlin: **There were the flicks, right near the Alexanderplatz. A long, narrow room stuffed to the gills, ghastly air, a breathless public. Workers, streetwalkers, pimps, above it all the sound of the schmaltzy, emotional commentary of the explainer, every word a lie. The film was actually frightfully boring, the banal story of a "girl of the people," called *The Woman without a Heart,* who is**

15

engaged to a young man of good family, is exposed in all her tawdriness, flees back into the arms of her first love, a worker, and is despised and rejected by him. Boring, right? But what they made of it! The explainer steamed with pure moral indignation, he mouthed the words of the dregs of the metropolis slowly and mawkishly, like a great delicacy. He explained the inner life of these characters, he completely captivated even me, or the activity of my brain, and suddenly you saw the "woman without a heart," a victim of the higher-ups, the poor worker, who they think is good enough to pick their lovers out of the filth of the gutter, the poor worker, a very model of honorable pride, who throws the girl back at the murderers on high—the social tragedy of every member of the audience, except that the ladies who were present had generally not made the detour via a counselor of commerce, but instead stayed right in the gutter... But this audience wants honorable workers and moralistic plots, only they must be against a background of brazen exploiters. The explainer sobbed, the audience clenched its fists, a tragedy sped by that was completely different from the one the film's manufacturer had seen... From the flicks will come the revolutions of the future. Every smarmy erstwhile comedian who croons this lucrative mishmash of coarseness and bombast about honor is Robespierre.

[12]

Max Brod mentions that he frequently visited the Orient and other establishments with his friend. Brod's interest in the cinema, however, is distinctly different from Kafka's. Brod takes what he has seen in the cinema and expands on it in his imagination; the enthusiastic viewer turns into an extravagant (script) writer. He understands cinema as an extension of literature, a process of assemblage. For Kafka, by contrast, the almost demonic technological element challenges the way we have learned to see, confronts the author's powers of sight and writing with very great, agonizing demands. Hence it is not surprising that Kafka is notably missing from Kurt Pinthus's *Book of the Cinema* published in 1913–14.

[13]

It may still be possible to describe in writing the quality of mechanical motion and exaltation that has been created in the field of aviation, or *locomotion aérienne*, as it appears simultaneously with the cinema; but when confronted by the latter's mechanically unrolling, trance-inducing images, writing threatens to be left behind. This is also the cause of the repeated, almost desperate cry to "Hold it!" as if the viewer has been attacked and is calling for help from writing, which brings it to a halt.

What is still possible in the case of the air show—participation in a great mechanical spectacle as a vision that embraces the spectators—dissolves, in the cinema, into incoherent momentary snapshots. It seems that versatile writing, even stenography, fails in the encounter with cinematography. Aviation, for all its technological bravura, is still an open-air "art," and its description lives from the immediate observation and inspired translation of the technological event that transpires in the heavens. Cinematography, by contrast, is a child of noctambulism.

In the fall of 1909, while on vacation in northern Italy, Kafka and the brothers Max and Otto Brod attend an air show in Brescia, which provides the occasion for Kafka's literarily and technically extremely inspired report "The Aeroplanes at Brescia," which appears on September 29 in the Prague daily *Bohemia*. With a fine sense for the rapid display of heavenly mechanical events all around him, Kafka sketches their enormous effect on the mass of fifty thousand spectators.

The semaphore tower indicates at once that the wind has become more favorable and that Curtiss will fly for the grand prize of Brescia. So he *is* starting, then? We scarcely agree about this, already Curtiss's motor is roaring, we scarcely look toward him, already he is flying away from us, flying across the plain, which grows larger in front of him, to the woods in the distance, which now seem to rise up for the first time. Long is his flight over those woods; he disappears, we are looking at the woods, not him. Behind some houses, God knows where, he reappears at the same altitude as before, races toward us; when he climbs, we see the lower surfaces of the biplane dipping darkly; when he sinks down, the upper surfaces glint in the sun. He comes around the semaphore tower and turns, oblivious to the din of the welcome, straightaway back where he came from, only to become rapidly small and lonesome again. 14

Kafka's postcard from Prague 1910

LES CORRESPONDENCES DOULOUREUSES,
OR THE PAVEMENT POUNDER

*Flâner. To go for a walk without any goal in mind, in accordance
with one's impulses and mood, to waste time uselessly. Etym. Of unknown origin.
However, Icelandic* flanni—*free-spirited—has been suggested.
Norman has* flanier—*stingy.*

Émile Littré, *Dictionnaire de la langue française*, 1876

*You read the brochures catalogs posters that sing out full-throatedly
That is the poetry of this morning and for prose we have the newspapers*

Guillaume Apollinaire, "Zone"

In the course of a generally arduous trip to Paris in October 1910, Kafka
experiences the metropolis—which he has long admired from afar—as a
grotesque, angst-inducing theater of decontextualization, a world in
which things are both turned on their heads and wrong-headed. Paris
dissolves into nonplaces, crossroads, metro stations, pure intensities
generated by mechanical acceleration. Kafka, always easily affected by
the "latest technology," experiences the unaccustomed turbulences physically. He has to interrupt the journey because of a boil that suddenly
erupts. Max and Otto Brod, his two traveling companions, remain
behind in Paris. Along with the dense, jotted-down notes of Max Brod,
who has already visited the (in every sense) "exemplary" city the previous
year, history has preserved a few pencilled notes by Kafka. In comparison
to his generally very intensive observations, it is a rather modest
account. A bit of text, a four-liner, jumps out at us from among the nota-
tions. The poem is written in French, and it is impossible to decide
whether Kafka wrote it himself or merely copied it down. The lapidary
tone allows more than one interpretation:

Front and back of a postcard from Kafka to Max Brod (addressed to Otto), showing a Paris street scene from 1910. The text of the card is translated beginning on P. 21.

Moi je flâne
qu'on m'approuve ou me condamne
je vois tout
je suis partout.

[As for me, I stroll / Let them commend me, or condemn me /
I see everything / I am everywhere.]

Once one has rid oneself of the assumption that the speaker here is a feeling, living entity, a psychic authority of one kind or another, and realizes that it may, instead, be a mechanical apparatus, for example a still or moving picture camera ("I see everything/am everywhere"), the four-liner, which seems to have been jotted down so casually, appears in a different light. It no longer appeals to a particular individual capacity to see or to an aesthetic preference but rather to anonymous "sights." The accelerated circulation, *le commerce des choses*, threatens to become an agony for the tourist if he exposes himself to the metropolis in such an unrestrained way. Kafka relates his boil directly to the actual bodily pain of being overwhelmed by Paris. This city gets under his skin—he is at its mercy, as the prisoner from "In the Penal Colony" is at the mercy of the graphological torture machine that writes itself into his body. The graphic ex- and impression of this torture are the three postcards that he combines into a letter-collage written from edge to edge on both sides and sends from Prague to the travelling companions who have remained in Paris:

Dear Max—

I arrived safely and only because I am regarded as an improbable phenomenon by everyone I am very pale. —The pleasure of shouting at the doctor was denied to me by a little fainting spell, which forced me onto his couch and during which—it was peculiar—I felt myself so very much a girl that I attempted to put my girl's skirt in order with my fingers. For the rest, the doctor declared that he was horrified by my appearance from the rear, the 5 new abscesses are no longer so important since a skin eruption has appeared that is worse than all abscesses, requires a long time to heal, and produces and will produce the actual pain. My idea, which I naturally did not betray to the doctor, is that this eruption was produced by the international sidewalks of Prague, Nuremberg, and especially, Paris. —So now I sit at home in the afternoon as if in a grave (I can't walk around on account of my plaster poultice, I can't sit still on account of the pain, which the healing makes even worse) and only in the morning do I emerge from this Beyond thanks to the office, to which I must go. Tomorrow I will go to your parents. —On the first night in Prague I dreamed, I think, the whole night through (sleep hung around this dream like a scaffold around a new building in Paris) that I had been lodged for sleeping in a large house that consisted of nothing except Paris horse cabs, automobiles, omnibuses, etc., which had nothing better to do than to drive close beside each other, past each other, over each other, and under each other and there was no talk or thought of anything but fares, connections, transfers, tips, *direction Pereire*, counterfeit currency, etc. On account of this dream I was

The great railroad strike of 1910. On October 13, four days after their arrival, Brod notes in his diary, "No electric light—strike—Gare du Nord," and in this lapidary way registers one of the most bitterly fought railroad strikes in French history. On Monday, October 10, 1910, the *cheminots* had voted for a strike that was intended to cut Paris off completely from the rest of France and to force the government to capitulate. On the following day, the Briand government ordered military personnel to replace the strikers. They succeeded in keeping some trains running. However, repeated acts of sabotage were committed against property belonging to the Interior Ministry. On Sunday, October 17, the discouraged railroaders—who had succeeded neither in expanding the strike into a general strike nor in gaining sufficient support even for their own strike among the general populace—voted to continue and expand the strike anyway; but the strike front broke down decisively at the beginning of the following week.

The tall man in the bowler hat (next to the Dubonnet advertisement) bears a startling resemblance to the Brod brothers' traveling companion. "Kafka to the train," notes Brod in his entry for this day. From *Max Brod, Franz Kafka: Eine Freundschaft*, 1: 38.

already unable to sleep, but since I wasn't properly informed about the necessary subjects, I was able to bear even the dreaming only with the greatest exertion. I complained inwardly that they had to lodge me, who was so much in need of rest after the journey, in such a house, but at the same time there was inside me an antagonist who, with the ominous bow of French doctors (they have buttoned-up work coats) admitted the necessity of this night. —Please count your money again whether I haven't robbed you, according to my not entirely fault-free accounting I have used so little that it looks as if I had spent the entire time in Paris bathing my wounds. Ugh, it hurts again. It was high time that I came back, for you and for me.

19   Your Franz K.

Paris impressed itself upon his body. He bears the sidewalk back to Prague like a martyr, and he "shows" his friends back in Paris, in calligraphic transcription, "his wounds" as the living im- and expression that Paris made upon him, his reading of the city, so to speak. These wounds and the bandages are his harvest, his very material impressions from the trip.

Paris is grasped by Kafka in the manner of cross-reading, much like the way Georg Christoph Lichtenberg experienced London. And like Lichtenberg, Kafka uses the "rear view mirror" of the three postcards—what a marvelously ironic reversal of the voyage, to send postcards from home to the tourists in Paris!—a fleeting picture of the metropolis, glimpsed in a dream, that further intensifies the impression of grotesque decontexualization.

Kafka's strolling, optically driven, ironically exaggerated, and derided ego extricates itself, writing, from the stiffness brought on by the bandages and the sidewalk. For Kafka, recollecting, Paris becomes the train that passes by—and rolls over him. But at the same time, it is the trace of writing, its pull, which releases him from the stupor. Cross-reading is the form of seeing that best befits his curious gaze, his exercises in sight and style. As he stumbles between a waking dream and a nightmare, the carefully maintained distinctions between the elevated (the *Bildungsreise* or educational tour) and the trivial (the pleasures of tourism) vanish as if of themselves. The word-pavement-plaster-postcards are playfully composed, artlessly artistic collages that mimetically overwrite his own pain—emphatically spelled-out messages to Paris, the paradise from which he has been prematurely and all-too-rapidly expelled.

The Kaiser Panorama

THE KAISER PANORAMA

I say that painting is worth that much more to me, the more it resembles bas relief,
and bas relief that much less, the more it resembles painting;
and so I always think of painting as the pale reflection of sculpture,
and the difference between the two as [between] moon and sun.

Michelangelo Buonarroti, 1547

23

They chased each other back and forth, and he chased the girl all the way into
the passage of the great bazaar where the Gaia Panorama was. Now it was closed,
naturally, but on the door you could see the listings of the next weeks' programs:
"Elephant Hunt in Africa," "Life in a Dutch Windmill."

Johannes Urzidil, *Die Verlorene Geliebte* (The Lost Beloved)

During an extended business trip from late January to early February 1911 to the prosperous northern Bohemian industrial cities of Friedland and Reichenberg, Kafka, looking for a way to pass the time, comes across an apparatus that was familiar to him from his youth in Prague. Kafka notes: **Kaiser Panorama. Sole entertainment in Friedland. Don't feel properly comfortable in it, because I had not expected such a handsome installation as I found there, had entered with snow-laden boots, and now, sitting in front of the eyepiece, barely touched the carpet with the tips of my toes. I had forgotten how the panoramas are arranged, and for a moment I was afraid I would have to go from chair to chair. An old man at a lamp-lit table, who is reading a copy of the *Illustrated World*, directs everything. After a little while plays an Ariston for me. Later 2 old women also enter, sit down to my right, then another one to my left. Brescia, Cremona, Verona. People inside like wax figures, their soles fixed to the ground on the sidewalk. Funerary monuments: a lady with a train trailing over a short flight of steps pushes a door slightly ajar and looks back as she does so.**

24

A family, in the foreground a young man is reading, his hand on his temple, a boy on the right draws a stringless bow. Monument to the hero Tito Speri: ragged and exuberant, his clothing drifts around his body. Peasant shirt, broad-brimmed hat. The scenes more alive than in the cinematograph, because they allow the eye the stillness of reality. The cinematograph lends the observed objects the agitation of their movement, the stillness of the gaze seems more important. Smooth floor of the cathedrals in front of our tongue. Why is there no combination of cinema and stereoscope in this way? Posters with Wihrer Pilsen familiar from Brescia. The distance between merely listening to a narrative and looking at a panorama is greater than the distance between the latter and looking at reality. Scrap iron market in Cremona. At the end wanted to tell the old man how much it had pleased me, didn't dare. Was handed the next program. Open from 10 o'clock to 10 o'clock.

Even before Kafka immerses himself fully in the apparatus, he takes note of an occurrence that is a strange kind of prelude to the mechanical movement that now commences. An old man, the attendant at the panorama, is reading the *Illustrated World*. Kafka himself, in a letter to his fiancée, once described this form of pure time-wasting, of reading, straying from the subject, and slowly leafing through, as a "huge, contradictory pleasure." The hand that turns the pages directs the entertainment, it creates a movement, a wave, into which the gaze can dive and from which it can resurface: "les mains feuillolent," says Apollinaire. The optically directed automatism of the hand is succeeded in the Kaiser Panorama by an automatism directed by the machine; the gaze of the viewer is fixed by the stereoscopic glasses. The viewer himself, as Kafka quickly remembers, remains at his place. Kafka describes the mechanical theater as a scene of frozen stillness into which he quite literally steps. The whole space is submerged in the (mechanical) sound of the Ariston. The sharp, clear scenes with their strange three-dimensionality remain before the eye of the viewer long enough to give him time to fully explore the imaginary space. But these photographs, as Kafka immediately realizes, are far removed from the "cinema," indeed, are diametrically opposed to it. Fundamentally, these are theatrically simulated scenes, images that proceed from the outside in, from the "fixed" figure to the background scenery, while the cinematic image, according to André Bazin, moves in the opposite, centrifugal direction. Kafka's eidetic

André Bazin: **Baudelaire writes, "The theater is a chandelier." If we had to find another symbol to counterpose this artificial crystal object, brilliant, multiple, and circular, which refracts the light rays around its center and holds us captive in its aureole, then we would say that film is the little electric torch of the usherette, which flashes like an uncertain comet across the darkness of our waking dream: the diffuse, ungeometrical, and unbounded space that surrounds the screen.**

memory helps him to hold fast to the images, which last only a few seconds, in a lively and detailed fashion.

In the midst of his observation, stimulated by the calm motion of the apparatus, Kafka digresses from the immediate description of the scenes and becomes aware of how disturbing the cinema's moving images are for his senses. The desired "combination of cinema and stereoscope" cannot exist—unless the film were to come to a halt and turn into a frozen tableau vivant. The motion picture, the image that moves while moving within itself, would have to stop in an unthinkable, undecidable movement somewhere between inside and outside. The three-dimensional standstill of stereoscopic photography makes the image *more alive*, in sharp contrast to the automatic agitation of the cinematic image, which is driven by movement—in the mechanical sense of a clock, as well—and infects the viewer with this movement, automates him. The lifelike quality that is imagined as being one of the characteristics of three-dimensional photography, however, has always been a determining characteristic of sculpture, of the plastic arts, which surpass all others in this respect. And it is sculpture and sculpturally observed spaces, above all, that Kafka conveys to us from his visit to the Kaiser Panorama.

The cinema, on the other hand, works against the stillness of the gaze and generates less a living than a mechanical reality, an automated unease. Seen from the motionless pole of the Kaiser Panorama, looking through a diaphanous image of remembrance (stereoscopic photography) at the living reality of sculpture, Kafka can think cinema as something different—and can speculate against it in writing. If there is an Archimedean point of rejection of cinematography, then it is here in Friedland, in the Kaiser Panorama, in the diary.

In the interior space of the images at which he gazes, as he observes the smooth floor of the cathedrals, Kafka stores up, indeed incorporates a future déjà vu: He ingests—"in front of our tongue"—photography like food. And when, two years later, he actually sets foot in the Gothic church of St. Anastasia in Verona and translates the sculpture of the dwarf that holds the baptismal font—a hunchbacked but happy little man—as the quintessence of his own despair, he can bring this image, which has penetrated him deeply in the past, back up into the light. The sculpture of the dwarf was already clearly recognizable in the Kaiser Panorama.

Kafka constructs what at first glance seems to be a strange, triadic relation of forces involving listening to a story about something, viewing a panorama, and seeing reality. Cinema has not disappeared from this relation, but instead, as a lesser level of the real, it is considered comparable to listening to a story. On the other hand, the realm of panorama-viewing, which is closer to *living* sculpture, has a higher reality content and is, to this extent, more closely related to seeing reality. But what this correlation reveals is not so much physiological processes that are being compared with each other as, rather, levels of literary perception that are being tried out. Kafka is a writer.

When he introduces the final scene, "Scrap Iron Market," it becomes clear that the entire description of the Kaiser Panorama is itself a kind of

Brescia, funerary monument to a widow.
Stereoscopic photograph from the Kaiser Panorama.

Verona, St. Anastasia. Stereoscopic photograph from the Kaiser Panorama.
The dwarf sculpture is at the lower right.

mimetic reflection of the apparatus. Kafka, following his observation and reflection, has folded and unfolded the text like a foldout album, a painted panorama in miniature. The time that elapses between one image and the next is mechanically articulated in such a way that the viewer has enough room to stray from the subject then dive back into the next motionless scene. The meter of the mechanism holds sway over thinking and writing—and the pauses between thoughts. The hours when the panorama is open suggest the circular joy of a miniature eternity in whose course "strange lands and peoples" pass before the young

30

"Körner's Death. Original drawing based on authentic reports." *Die Gartenlaube*, 1863.

Kafka to Felice Bauer, night of January 17–18, 1913: **I have now, dearest, for the first time in a long time, spent a lovely hour reading again. You would never guess what I have read and what has caused me such pleasure. It was an old issue of the *Gartenlaube* (Gazebo) from the year 1863. I didn't read anything in particular, but leafed slowly through 200 pages, examined the (at that time, due to the costly reproduction, rare) images, and only here and there read something of particular interest. Time and again I am drawn to older eras in this fashion, and the pleasure of experiencing human relations and ways of thinking in a complete, yet still wholly understandable version (my God, 1863, that was only fifty years ago); in spite of this no longer being able to experience them in detail, from below, emotionally, and hence being confronted with the need to play with them according to my mood and fancy—this contradictory pleasure, for me, is tremendous. Time and again, I like to read old newspapers and journals. And this old, heart-wrenching, expectant Germany from the middle of the previous century! The modest circumstances, the closeness that each person feels to others, the publisher to the subscriber, the writer to the reader, the reader to the great writers of the period (Uhland, Jean Paul, Seume, Rückert, "Germany's bards and Brahmins").** For more on Körner, see PP. 61–65.

employee as if in a piano piece by Robert Schumann. *Illustrated World* is the name of the waking dream that is being performed here, uninterruptedly: "Open from 10 o'clock to 10 o'clock."

In a metaphorical sense, the cyclically constructed Kaiser Panorama is an image of Kafka's Italian journey. We may confidently suppose that the old man who leafs through the *Illustrated World* is a metamorphosis of the kaiser whose two given names, Franz and Joseph, are linked with

Kafka's own name and that of a character in his novels. And how *could* he "dare" to speak to the kaiser?

The panorama of northern Italy, stretching from Venice to Verona, was either already familiar to Kafka—as in the case of Brescia and Riva—or he would come to know it during the years leading up to the outbreak of the world war. In fact, when he heads south, his eye and he himself always skirt the boundaries of the Habsburg Empire, which until 1859 extended deep into the northern Italian peninsula. He will never transgress this southern border, whose most distant points the Kaiser Panorama lets pass before his eyes.

Still showing the female slave trader and her captive from *The White Slave Girl* 1911

THAT WHITE
SLAVE GIRL AGAIN

*To sit in a railroad carriage, forget it, live as if at home, suddenly remember, feel the power
of the train rushing forward, become a traveler, pull one's cap from the valise,
greet one's fellow travelers more freely, cordially, urgently, be borne undeservedly toward
the destination, feel this like a child, become a favorite of the ladies, be under the
constant attractive power of the window, always leave at least an outstretched hand resting
on the windowsill. Even more precisely sized-up situation: to forget that you have forgotten,
at one stroke, in the lightning train, become a child traveling alone around
whom the train car, trembling with haste, assembles itself astonishingly in the
tiniest of things, as if from the hand of a juggler.*

Kafka, *Diary*, July 31, 1917

The cinema is the diary of modern life.

G. A. de Caillavet, 1912

On February 25, 1911, in other words, immediately after his return from
the business trip to northern Bohemia, Kafka dispatches a quick note to
Max Brod, his friend and correspondent. There is one passage in the letter
that stands out among the general news of the day: **Some news, dear
Max: people have already heard thrushes singing in the Volksgarten
Park—the palace carriages, when the fine ladies and gentleman dis-
embark, have to be held down behind on account of the powerful
springs—today on my way here I saw a duck in the water standing at
the edge of the river—I rode with a woman who strongly resembled
the female slave trader from *The White Slave Girl*, etc.** Kafka is in fine
fettle. Together with his friend, in Prague, he has evidently seen the film
The White Slave Girl, which was announced with great fanfare.

This *White Slave Girl* is the third remake of a Danish film subject that
was brought out again and again with great success—and was labeled
an absolute *Schundfilm*, or trash film—and always with the same theme:
a young woman, without resources, is lured away from her homeland

and forced into prostitution in a foreign country. After a dramatic search, the rejected lover or fiancé succeeds in freeing her—already dishonored, he believes—from the clutches of the slave-trader.

Now, there is nothing unusual about seeing in chance acquaintances actors who are familiar from film or photographs, or about identifying one particular face, from among the masses of anonymous faces that flash by every day, with the "familiar" face of the actor, as long as one's own desire and the formal resemblance are sufficiently great. But this "film acquaintance" of Kafka's is a story all its own.

The story revolves around two women, the apparently solicitous, in reality sadistic, slave trader, on the one hand, and Edith, the "innocent heroine," on the other. First, Kafka is riding with the evil female lead, then six months later with the "innocent heroine," daydreaming and corresponding about his daydream.

In late August 1911, the friends set out on another big journey. It lasts the better part of a month, from August 26 to September 20, and takes them from Prague via Pilsen and Munich to Lindau; from there via St. Gallen and Winterthur to Zurich; then over the Gotthard Pass to Lugano. On September 4, they arrive in Milan, where in addition to the bordello Al Vero Eden they pay two visits to the Teatro Fossati and take in the cathedral and other sights. On September 7, they continue on via St. Moritz, Montreux, Lausanne, and Dijon to Paris. They remain in Paris, which they explore indefatigably and with unflagging curiosity, until September 13. They return home by separate routes.

From this voyage we have not only Kafka's and Brod's diaries (and several essays by Brod) but also the draft of a joint novelistic treatment: *Richard and Samuel*. This project was broken off after the first chapter, but the surviving fragment provides us with a lively episode from the beginning of the trip.

It is not just a *Bildungsreise*, educational tour, in the traditional sense. Armed with the "red guardian," as Rudolf Borchard scornfully described the scarlet-bound Baedeker, they set about outdoing Baedeker with their own travel guide—it was to be called *Cheap*. It is also a voyage in images. Images of advertising placards, panoramas, and postcards; images from museums and special newspaper sections; and, not last, cinematic images literally riddle the diary pages of the two graphomaniacs. Visual stimuli, stimulating images abound wherever they cast their eyes—and where the reader's eye is led. In the midst of the running commentary from Milan, Kafka, unsparing when it came to himself, noted: "Irresponsible to travel without taking notes, even to live. The deathly sense of the monotonous passing of the days is impossible." Of his diligently shorthand-taking friend he notes critically and with admiration, "Max regrets what he has written only during the process of writing; afterwards, never."

It is the last great bachelor journey. Max Brod gets engaged in 1912 — "engaged away," Kafka calls it in a moment of jealousy in a letter to Felice. And hence this journey is still completely under the sign of true male friendship. "A married friend is no friend," Kafka will confide to his diary in 1914.

From the beginning, it is evident that the two share an extraordinary kinetic enjoyment, the pleasure they take in traveling by train, taxi, or subway, and in experiencing these means of conveyance — as will be shown in Munich — rather like a "traveling" camera on a dolly. Max Brod notes: **In Pilsen a lady enters the railway carriage… The lady is Angela Rehberger, the daughter of a military officer. Makes our acquaintance thanks to the fact that her big hat in its box falls or floats softly down onto my head. Wagnerian. Collects chocolate wrappers; but cigar bands too. Is traveling to Trient to her parents. Works all day long in a technical bureau, is very contented with her life. Takes iron, since she has been ill… In Munich automobile ride through the city. Night and rain. We see, of all edifices, only the first floor, since the car's big visor blocks our view. Fantastic imaginings of the height of the palaces and churches. Perspective of a basement apartment, says Kafka.** `34`

Kafka recognizes the situation and establishes the perspective. *His* perspective. He seconds and deepens his friend's description; although he is driving through the city at street level, he imagines himself in the basement. He associates the sound of the rain-soaked tires with the mechanical hissing of a projector. And finally, he compares the office girl — first cautiously, then more and more vehemently — with the cliché of a movie character who has evidently had a powerful impact on him. Kafka: **Rain, fast drive (20 min.), perspective of a basement apartment, driver calls out the names of the invisible sights, the tires hiss on the asphalt like the apparatus in the cinematograph, the most distinct thing: the uncurtained windows of the Four Seasons, the reflection of the streetlights in the asphalt as in a river.** `35`

Stills from the kidnapping scene
of *The White Slave Girl*.

Apart from the verbal hijinks of the "invisible sights," fabricated in the
spirit of Karl Valentin, what is sketched here is the décor of a very particular seduction scene. In the first chapter of the jointly conceived novel
Richard and Samuel—it was eventually meant to bear the subtitle *A Little
Voyage through Parts of Central Europe*—the story, prudently displaced
into the realm of fiction, is more brightly lit. Kafka's alias "Richard" evidently assumes the role of the guilty conscience, while Brod's alias
"Samuel" is allowed to appear all the more uninhibitedly as the seducer

and then as the deceiver deceived. Angela or Alice Rehberger turns into "Dora Lippert" in the novel.

Brod notes: **Well, uniforms don't impress her at all, and officers are nothing in her eyes. Evidently part of the blame for this belongs to the gentleman who lends her the piano scores but partly also to our stroll back and forth on the platform of the railway station in Furth, for after the trip she feels so refreshed by the stroll and strokes her hips with the palms of her hands.**

Kafka seconds him: **Dora L. has round cheeks with a lot of blonde down on them, but they are so bloodless that one would have to press one's hands against them for a long time before a blush would begin to show. The bodice is poor; above its edge the blouse wrinkles on the breast; one would have to ignore it... I compliment her; she is so musical. Samuel, for his part, seems to smile ironically as she sings something to him under her breath. Perhaps it was not quite correct, but after all, is it not deserving of admiration that a single girl in a big city takes such a heartfelt interest in music?... Only now do we learn that she is not entirely well, was even sick in bed for a long time... Indeed, the cause of her anemia was clear to me from the very start. The office. One can take office life, like everything else, in a light-hearted way (and this girl honestly does take it that way, indeed is completely deceived), but in essence, in the unhappy consequences? —After all, I know what situation I, for example, am in. And now even a girl is supposed to sit in an office, a woman's skirt is not at all made for this, how it must pull everywhere to be constantly pushed back and forth for hours on a hard wooden chair. And that is how these round derrières are pressed down, and the breast simultaneously against the edge of the desk— do I exaggerate?—A girl in an office is always a sad sight for me after all.**

The meaning or, expressed more cautiously, the purpose of this practically anatomical approach is not to "get close" to Dora Lippert in any crass sense but rather to imagine her away from the hated sphere of the office, indeed, to retouch her, *peu à peu*, out of crude reality altogether and to entrust her to the realm of pure, cinematic fiction. In the next scene—the trio has meanwhile arrived in Munich and "Samuel has already become rather intimate with her"—he allows Dora herself to speak for herself for the first time. And what she says sounds like the intertitle of a melodrama. It is the musical fräulein's aria as told by the

36

"explainer": **This Samuel has persuaded her, despite her lively resistance, which is supported by the downpour, to take advantage of the half-hour stopover in Munich for an automobile ride. While he goes to fetch a car, she tells me, in the railway station arcade, and takes me by the arm: "Please, prevent this trip. I cannot go with you. It is quite out of the question. I am telling you this because I trust you. It is impossible to talk to your friend. He is so crazy!" —We climb in; for me the whole thing is embarrassing, it also reminds me precisely of the cinematograph piece *The White Slave Girl*, in which just outside the railway station, in the dark, the innocent heroine is hustled into an automobile by strange men and taken away. Samuel, on the other hand, is in a good mood.**

"We climb in." The projector is running, and as in the ride with the female slave dealer half a year earlier, the blending of the real with the fictional takes the form of a fade-over or double exposure *during the trip itself.* Like Fräulein Rehberger alias Dora Lippert in the railway carriage and then in the taxi, the unknown woman in the streetcar is linked to the cinematic fiction. Franz Kafka traces the reality of the night in Munich through the cinematic night of the film scene—it had been colored dark blue—onto the pages of his diary. Thus the action—this by no means nonviolent scene—is "fixed." The writer succeeds by this very particular process in redeeming, or catching up with, the very thing that he has always complained about in regard to the images that run away and escape from him. Here Kafka is able to "hold fast" to the images and to the fräulein as well. The tiny strip of film, the little scene in which the "innocent heroine" leaves the railway station lasts all of three seconds in the copy that has come down to us today.

There is certainly also something quite different at issue here than Kafka's phenomenal eidetic memory, when he happens to recall precisely this very rapidly vanishing scene, which flashed by so quickly and is really not an episode but merely a transition, a passage, a little transformation. He stops the scene with the help of his extensive description, and he transforms it gently, but precisely; he nudges it in a slightly different direction and in so doing he is able to dissolve "his" innocent heroine, Dora, into the fiction.

In the film scene, the innocent heroine, pursued by the slave trader, leaves the railway station and walks toward a waiting taxi. Just as she is about to reach the taxi, her path is crossed by two men who are also heading toward it. For a split second a small crowd gathers, which disperses as if of its own accord as soon as the heroine and her companion have gotten into the taxi. Unharassed and untroubled by the men, the taxi begins to move and roars off. The "strange men" who harass her and carry her off did not exist at all in that form.

Kafka transforms the two men who suddenly appear on camera and cross paths with the two women into kidnappers, even pimps. And in this transformation, he himself enters the scene with Max. Thus modified, the cinematic recollection inserts itself perfectly into the "real" encounter at the Munich railway station and into the enforced taxi ride. Kafka projects the film scene—slightly retouched—onto the real event in Munich and unburdens himself of the reality, which he evidently experiences as oppressive: "For me the whole thing is embarrassing."

As soon as this artful double exposure has been made, the taxi ride, which hums along as mechanically as clockwork, like a projector (for projecting the invisible sights), can leave embarrassing or tormenting reality behind—and become cinema. Pure kinetic, cinematographic, and graphomatic pleasure; the enjoyment of the sheer unadulterated passivity in which the bodies and senses of the three passengers are borne through the rain-drenched, illuminated night. What they see are "invisible sights", and what they hear is the hissing of the apparatus in the cinematograph.

They see it from a basement perspective, the K-perspective or Kafka perspective, one not dissimilar from the perspective of the cinema. And the melodrama taking shape in the taxi between the seducer from the provinces and the innocent heroine satisfies all the erotic and sexual clichés that the primitive films of the genre served up.

Kafka writes this up like an experienced moviegoer and traveling companion. **It is night. Perspectives of a basement apartment. Samuel, on the other hand, comes up with fantastic imaginings of the height of the palaces and churches. Since Dora in her shadowy seat, facing backward, is still silent and I almost fear there will be an outburst, he finally becomes baffled and asks her, rather conventionally for my taste, "Now, you are not mad at me, are you, fräulein? Have I done anything to you," etc.? She responds, "Since I happen to be here I will not spoil your pleasure. But you shouldn't have tried to force me. When I say, 'No,' I am not saying it for no reason. I may not go for a ride." "Why?" he asks. "I cannot tell you that. You yourself**

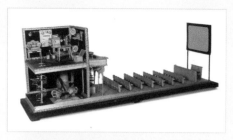

Plywood model of a Prague silent film cinema (CA. 1930). The most expensive seats were in the back, "in the interest of the public."

The K-perspective. Advertisement for *Der Kinematograph* (The Cinematograph), "publication for the entire art of projection."

must understand that is it not proper for a girl to go out driving with gentlemen at night. There is something else besides. Just assume for a moment that I were already promised…" We guess, each for himself, with unspoken respect, that this business has something to do with the Wagner fellow. Well, I have nothing to reproach myself for but try to cheer her up all the same. Samuel, who has treated her a bit condescendingly until now, also seems to feel regret and now only wants to talk about the journey.

And intoxicatingly, with the hiss of real tires in the background and outfitted with an "explainer" of the most sophisticated kind, the scene glides over into pure cinema. As Kafka imagines it, it is pure wish fulfillment, which naturally could not have been crowned with success in the taxi, at night, with the three of them, and would probably also have been embarrassing. In the film, however, in Kafka's film, the "driver, at our request, …calls out the names of the invisible sights. The tires hiss on the asphalt like the apparatus in the cinematograph. Once again, that 'white slave girl.'"

A Munich swaddled in sound, viewed from the K-perspective, glides by the three travelers. Fräulein Dora no longer sings. And it is not surprising that in this state even the most familiar things suddenly appear strange, or that the young man humming along in a mechanical wish-conveyance, in a bachelor machine in twenty-minute ecstasy, cannot explain to himself where this strangeness comes from: **Only at the Freiheitsmonument, with its fountains plashing in the rain, are we** allowed to remain a little longer. Bridge over the—only suspected—Isar River. Lovely manorial villas lining the English Garden. Ludwig Strasse, Theatiner Church, Field Marshall Hall, Pschorr Brewery. I don't know how it happens: I don't recognize a thing, although after all I have already been in Munich several times. Sendlinger Gate. Railway station, where I was concerned (above all on Dora's account) about arriving in time. So we hummed through the city in all of twenty minutes, like a spring that was set precisely to arrive there, according to the taxi meter.

39

The trick of transforming real shame into the unreal shamelessness of the cinema has brushed off the embarrassment of the forcible persuasion to the nocturnal ride. Unharassed and safely preserved, Fräulein Dora is delivered to a lady who awaits her on the train to Innsbruck. And Kafka, after having survived the affair, and the taxi, as an irreproachable young bachelor, cannot resist identifying the individual who has just entered the scene with the meanwhile familiar cinematic character from *The White Slave Girl*. It is, if we go by his description, the fear-inducing slave trader from the film, the black-clad Other with whom he has already had the virtual pleasure of riding a year previously: "We stow our Dora, as if we were her Munich relatives, in a carriage bound for Innsbruck, where a black-clad lady, who is more to be feared that we, offers her protection for the night."

40

Max Brod sustained a few wounds in the affair. In contrast to his friend, he had most likely gone too far in pursuing the real Dora, and after he failed to achieve his aim he was all-too-outspoken in denying that this had been the case. Kafka's special trick, to deprive the scene of its reality by translating it into cinema, evidently remained obscure to him. Indeed, he does not even seem to have noticed this displacement of Kafka's when they transcribed it in their collaborative novel.

In the end, Max Brod is forced to carry the burden of shame alone. He writes, **The affair with Dora was a failure through and through. The further it went, the worse. My aim was to interrupt the voyage and spend the night in Munich. Until suppertime, Regensburg Station, more or less, I was convinced it would succeed. I tried to communicate with Richard by means of a few words on a scrap of paper. He did not even seem to have read it, concerned only to put it out of sight. Ultimately, it is nothing, I had no desire at all for the insipid young lady. Only Richard made such a fuss over her, with his long-winded**

41

Max Brod on Kafka:
He loved the earliest films, which appeared at that time. He was especially delighted with a film that in Czech was called *Táta Dlouhán*, **which could probably be translated as** *Daddy Longlegs*. **He dragged his sisters to this film, later me, always with great enthusiasm, and for hours at a time he could not be made to talk about anything else but precisely and only about this splendid film.**
Max Brod, *Streitbares Leben. Autobiographie* (Pugnacious Life. An Autobiography; Munich, 1960), 274. Here Kafka was referring to the Marshal A. Neilan film *Daddy-Long-Legs* (1919), Kafka himself never mentions it, but the drunken dog is so monstrous that he must have been impressed by it.

speeches and pleasantries. This encouraged her in her stupid affecta-
tion, which finally became completely unbearable in the automobile.
When we said good-bye, consequently, she turned into a sentimental German Gretchen. Richard, who naturally carried her valise,
behaved as if she had made him undeservedly happy; I only had a
feeling of embarrassment.

Kafka leaves Brod standing in the rain. The latter looks on during his
friend's "long-winded speeches and pleasantries" and does not notice

that Kafka has long since turned on the projector. He doesn't need to read the scrap of paper with Brod's whispered intertitles—Dora herself will provide them for him. The person who, like Brod, lets himself be completely carried away by the seduction scene that he has set up, without being aware of the (relief-bringing) escape route into fiction, will at least—if he does not have to do penance for it—have to suffer alone the embarrassment that at the beginning of the scene had still been entirely Kafka's. This day did not pass "monotonously"!

The White Slave Girl belongs to the genre of films that legitimizes a shamefacedly shameless peek into the bordello. The scandal, for conservative anticinema circles, lay precisely in the fact that film offers this (in)sight, and in the process shows the bordello as a place that is not merely infamous. A particular point made by The White Slave Girl, by the way, was the fact that she defended herself against the advances of her pimp by means of her own strength, by strangling him. In the opinion of the cultivated moderate bourgeoisie, it was showing sexuality that was the crime. In the extensive Czech critique of the film one gains a sense of the special infamy of this film, which in spite or because of its scathing moralizing reviews was enjoyed sotto voce.

Illustration, front page, *La Domenica del Corriere* 1911

PARIS IN DOTTED LINES,
OR THE THEFT OF THE MONA LISA

My life here is as if I were quite certain of a second life, the way, for example,
I got over the pain of the failed sojourn in Paris by thinking that I would seek
to come there again soon. Meanwhile, the sight of the sharply etched patches
of light and shadow on the cobblestone streets.

Kafka, *Diary*, February 21, 1911

There are an amazing number of movie theaters. On the boulevards
they are chock-a-block, one garishly colored poster follows the next, and in the
evening hours the illuminated advertising is entirely on their account.
The Parisians will certainly soon have arrived at the point where they can see
everything they have read in the latest newspaper immediately in the cinema as well.

"Erste Internationale Film-Zeitung," November 23, 1912

Milan welcomes the two travelers in early September 1911 with cholera warnings and a large, colorful title page on the Sunday supplement to the *Corriere della Sera*: the theft of the *Mona Lisa* from the Louvre. The theft had occurred on August 21, and the flood of images and news reports that it unleashed will follow them on their journey from now on.

The real substrate of *The White Slave Girl* — prostitution — is sought out in the bordello Al Vero Eden; the initials may be a parodistic echo of the initials of the royal name of the Galleria Vittorio Emmanuele, where the establishment was located.

One almost has the impression as if Kafka is withdrawing into his writing in order to transmit anatomical-erotic signals that emanate from the *girls*. They read like captions for the still photos that an anonymous Paris police inspector had taken around 1900: **The girl, whose belly, when she sat, was undoubtedly shapeless above and between the wide-stretched legs under the gauzy frock, while when she stood up it vanished, like a theater decoration behind scrims, and formed**

45

an ultimately tolerable girl's body. The French girl, whose sweetness the conclusive look discovered, above all, in the plump and yet detailed, chatty and affectionate knees.

The stillness of the gaze that Kafka discovered in the Kaiser Panorama can be fully developed during the visit to the Teatro Fossati. It was probably not the Lombard dialect in which the plays and operettas were presented that drew the two not merely culture-hungry tourists back for a second visit. Kafka's calmly cheerful stenographic jottings lead us through the passagelike interior of the theater, which lay perpendicular to its two entrances, between the Corso Garibaldi and the Via Rivoli. The orchestra, at the same level as the public, served to heighten the impression of a great, uncomplicated proximity to the events on stage. The stage was brightly lit, at its center [stood] the illuminated actor. "The theater is a chandelier," says Baudelaire.

Kafka lets his gaze wander through the large space and finally focuses his entire concentration on the peculiar appearance of the actor: **Theatro Fossati—all hats and fans in motion—laughter of a child high above—program pasted over with an advertising flyer—an elderly lady in the male orchestra—*Poltrone—Ingresso*—orchestra on the same level as the audience—advertisement for Lancia included in the ceiling décor of one of the salons—all the windows along the back wall open—great strong actor with delicately crosshatched nostrils, whose blackness remains noticeably present even when the borders of the face, bent backwards, dissolve in the light.**

The great strong actor is none other than the—at that time very popular—Edoardo Ferravilla, who enjoyed triumphal success during the entire month of September as Don Romeo in the local Lombard play *Le Dot d'on ceregh* (The Dowry of an Acolyte).

As they continue their journey toward Stresa, Kafka notes the "bas-relief-like movements of the sleepers in the full carriage"—a nice image for the apparently flattened bodies and faces of the travelers, sitting sideways.

Paris, the goal of their journey, is perambulated, driven through, gaped at, wondered over, sightseen and written about to the point of exhaustion. As if conducting an on-site revision of the four-liner from the previous Paris trip, Kafka unfolds the rapidly changing urban views like a fan. And like a "cubist," he pastes together trivial and sublime objects in a montage that gives a new picture of the city that, as we know according to Brod, is "exemplary in every way": **the characteristic surface formats: shirts, laundry altogether, napkins in the restaurant, sugar, large wheels of the usually 2-wheeled carts, horses harnessed one behind the other, flatish steamboats on the Seine, the balconies bisect the houses horizontally and broaden these surface sections of the houses, the chimneys pressed flat, the newspapers folded together**

Paris in dotted lines: the flat chimneys sprouting tall thin chimneys (with the numerous small flower-pot-like ones), the extremely silent old gas chandeliers, the horizontal lines of the Venetian blinds, to which are added, in the suburbs, dotted lines of dirt on the walls of the buildings, the narrow railings on the roofs we saw in the Rue Rivoli, the dotted lines on the glass roof of the Grand Palais des Art [sic], the windows outside the shop interiors intersected by lines, the grille-work of the balconies, the Eiffel Tower composing itself of lines, the even more powerful linear effect of the outer and inner moldings on the balcony doors opposite our windows, the little outdoor chairs and the little café tables, whose legs are lines, the gold-tipped grille-work fences of the public gardens. 48

The world is "dotted," artfully shaded, and crosshatched even for the person who has emerged from the confines of the cinema. Or for the person who drives through a nocturnally rainy, illuminated city. The dotted-line rain is the cinematic foil, the projection behind which the city is perceived.

During the late-night drive through Munich, Kafka had noted down the catchword of the "invisible sights," the most significant and newsworthy of which will now be the object of "sightseeing" in Paris. Like an advertising flyer in the literal sense, the theft of the *Mona Lisa*, multiply refracted in images and news reports, has run on ahead of them. Once in Paris, they waste no time in seeking out the site of the crime, in order, in the company of numerous other curious visitors, to stare at the empty space on the wall of the Louvre where the famous lady had hung until August 21, 1911. Evidently finding the sensation value greater than the embarrassment, the directors of the Louvre exhibited the "mark of shame," the empty wall, to visitors for several weeks.

The very next day, on September 10, the two Paris tourists find themselves marveling at a parody of the shameful event in the giant Omnia Pathé movie hall. Max Brod recorded the evening: 49

On the very evening that we had set aside as a night off, after so

Stills from *Nick Winter and the Theft of the Mona Lisa*.

many nocturnal exertions, for a modest meal in the four walls of our hotel and early to bed, we chanced upon a doorway on the boulevard, decked out with little electric light bulbs and a not exactly energetic barker, whose cap, however, bore a title that attracted us more magically than all his words could have. Omnia Pathé... So here we stood at the source of so many of our enjoyments, once more at the center of a business whose rays shone so powerfully over the whole world that one would almost rather not believe in the existence of a center—a feeling, by the way, that was typical for our Parisian mood; for powerful central firms (like Pneu Michelin, Douçet, Roger Gallet, Clement Bayard, etc.) besiege the heart of the newcomer with surprising force. We again dispensed with the night off (damned city!) and went in.

It is hard for one darkened hall to differentiate itself from other darkened halls. But for us, who are always firmly set on finding in everything Parisian something special and better than anyplace else, we are soon struck by the spaciousness—no, that's not it yet—then, that people are disappearing through a dark doorway in the background and a cool draft seems to regulate this continuous movement of the audience—no, that's how it is at home, too, uninterrupted showings, an entrance and an exit door—but now we feel we are on firmer ground. This freedom of people to be able to position themselves anywhere there is room, even in the aisle between the rows of benches, even on the ramp in the background that leads up to the apparatus, indeed, even next to the apparatus, is something decidedly republican, any police force other than the Parisian police would not approve of it. Equally republican, we must admit, is the freedom of the many columns in the hall to be allowed to disturb the audience's view in whatever way they please...

A girl in the uniform of a soldier in an operetta, on her cap, this time, the ambiguous inscription "Omnia," accompanies us to our seats, sells us an (according to good Parisian custom, inexact) program. And already we are under the spell of the blindingly white, trembling screen in front of us. We nudge each other. "Say, the show *is* better here than at home." Naturally, after all, in Paris everything has to be better.

50

Then Brod describes in detail the five-minute sketch "Nick Winter et le vol de la Joconde": At the end, after the usual revolver shots, chases, fisticuffs, came the news. Naturally she was not absent—the one you now see on all the advertisements, candy boxes, and postcards in Paris: *Mona Lisa*. The picture opened with the presentation of M. Croumolle (everyone knows that it means "Homolle," and no one protests against the perfidious way they are going after the gray-haired Delphi scholar). Croumolle is lying in bed, his stocking cap pulled down over his ears, and is startled out of sleep by a telegram: "*Mona Lisa* Stolen." Croumolle—the Delphi scholar, if you please, but

51

Inside the Omnia Pathé.

I am not protesting, I was laughing so hard—dresses himself with clownlike agility, now he puts both feet into one leg of his pants; now one foot into two socks. In the end, he runs into the street with his suspenders trailing, all the bystanders turn around to look at him, even those who are far in the background and evidently not in the pay of Pathé... It is a longing that ever since the emergence of the cinema lives on in me with the force of my early childhood wishes— I would like just once, by chance, to turn a street corner where such a staged cinematographic scene is taking place. What wouldn't it be possible to improvise there! And in any case, what a sight!... But to continue. The story is set in the hall of the Louvre, everything excellently imitated, the paintings and, in the middle, the three nails on which the *Mona Lisa* hung. Horror; summoning of a comical detective; a shoe button of Croumolle's as red herring; the detective as shoeshine boy; chase through the cafés of Paris; passers-by forced to have their shoes shined; arrest of the unfortunate Croumolle, for the button that was found at the scene of the crime naturally matches his shoe buttons. And now the final gag—while everyone is running through the hall at the Louvre and acting sensational, the thief sneaks in, the *Mona Lisa* under his arm, hangs her back where she belongs, and takes Velázquez's *Princess* instead. No one notices him. Suddenly someone sees the *Mona Lisa*; general astonishment, and a note in one corner of the rediscovered painting that says, 'Pardon me, I am nearsighted. I actually wanted to have the painting next to it." ... Croumolle, poor man, is released.

52

In the course of a systematic search of the labyrinthine rooms of the Louvre, in the staircase that leads to the Cour Visconti, much too late, they discovered the frame and the bulletproof glass that were meant to protect the *Mona Lisa* from "vandals"...

The film, evidently, took aim not only at the director of the Louvre, Homolle, but also at France's leading criminologist, Bertillon. The latter had already thoroughly compromised himself in the Dreyfus case, when he prepared a graphological certificate implicating Dreyfus that later proved to be erroneous. On August 24, 1911, Bertillon discovered the print of a left thumb on the frame of the *Mona Lisa*, whereupon the entire staff of the Louvre, including the director, was fingerprinted.

In his essay, Max Brod also describes the other films that were shown that evening at the Omnia Pathé: **We saw, indeed we saw a great deal—by analogy to the Comédie, which puts eight acts on stage almost without intermission. We saw the doctor visit the poor sick child and turn around melodramatically several times in the doorway, with a distinctly pitying expression. We saw the mercifulness of some English king or other, hand-colored, sandwiched between some theatrical armor and a ruin (which had been created from a burned-out suburban cottage), enjoying life... Then, in addition, the *Journal Pathé*. And so that everything quite resembles a newspaper, the title page and "Year III" are solemnly projected beforehand. We see demonstrations against inflation in France, which look like they have been arranged by Pathé; everyone is grinning in the direction of the audience.**

53

At the end, Kaiser Wilhelm rides across the screen, and Brod closes his essay with a comparison between French and foreign pomp.

The visit to the cinema is one of a series of *Augenblicksbeobachtungen*, momentary observations or snapshots, which are the virtually uninterrupted preoccupation of the two bachelors during their voyage. Only on rare occasions does Kafka's travel diary pause, as, for example, when he minutely describes an accident involving a tricycle rider and an automobile, or when—recalling the failed sojourn of the previous year—he now lets himself be transported through Paris by the Métro with evidently greater élan, and the nightmare that pursued him at that time from correspondence to *correspondence* now gives way to a more peaceful vision. Traffic in its pure form, moving smoothly and wordlessly, allows the stranger to penetrate the essence of Paris. **Horrific was the din of the Métro when I rode it, for the first time in my life, from Montmartre to the big boulevards. Otherwise it is not bad, even intensifies the pleasant, calm feeling of speed. The advertisement for Dubonnet is suitable to be read, anticipated, and observed by sad and unoccupied passengers. Exclusion of language from transit, since one does not need to speak either when paying or when entering and leaving. The Métro, thanks to its ease of comprehension, is the best opportunity for the eager but weakly stranger to acquire the belief that on his first attempt he has penetrated into Paris properly and rapidly.**

Only a few days after the end of the journey and struggling with obvious difficulties in advancing the project of the joint novel, Kafka is reading Goethe's diaries and reflecting on the change in perception that is brought about for the traveler by technology, speed, and the straightened-out landscape: **Travel observations of Goethe different from those of today, because, made from a stagecoach with the slow changes in terrain, they develop more simply and can be followed much more easily even by the person who does not know those parts. A peaceful, literally landscapelike thinking occurs. Since the landscape offers itself to the passengers in the coach undamaged, in its inborn character, and the highways, too, cut through the countryside much more naturally than the stretches of railroad, to which the highways are perhaps related as rivers are to canals; hence there is no need for acts of violence on the part of the onlooker, either, and he can see systematically without effort. Therefore, there are few momentary observations, usually only in interior spaces where certain people immediately burst in precipitously right in front of one's eyes.**

The left-hand photograph is from an unpublished compilation of nearly eighty photos of bordellos that were prepared at the behest of an unknown Paris police inspector under the title "Les maisons de tolérance, de passes et de rendez-vous." The collection is now in the possession of the Bibliothèque Nationale. On the right, a still from *The White Slave Girl*.

The reading matter seems perfectly suited to legitimate, after the fact, the description of a Paris "in dotted lines" that dissolves into its individual details. In the process, Kafka's "momentary observations" emit splinters as sharp as the description of the visit to a Paris bordello, which exposes with photographic clarity the atmosphere that in *The White Slave Girl* had been muffled in bashful kitsch. **Rationally organized bordello. The sheer Venetian blinds of the tall windows of the entire establishment lowered. In the doorman's box instead of a man a respectably dressed woman who could be at home anywhere. Already in Prague I have always, in passing, noticed the Amazon-like character of the bordellos. Here it is even more evident. The female doorman who presses her electrical bell, who restrains us in her box because she is told that at that moment guests are descending the stairs, the two respectably dressed women upstairs (why two?), who receive us, the turning up of the electric light in the next room, in which the unoccupied girls were sitting in the dark or semidark, the three-quarter circle (we complete it to make a circle) in which they stand in poses thought to be advantageous, the big step with which the chosen one steps forward, the grip of the madam with which she summons me... Impossible for me to imagine how I arrived at the street, so quick was it. It is difficult to get a more detailed look at the girls there, because they are too numerous, blink with their eyes, above all stand too** close. One would have to open one's eyes wide, and this requires practice. I actually remember only the one who stood directly in front of me. She had gaps in her teeth, stood tall, held her dress together with a fist clenched over her private parts and opened and closed her big eyes and big mouth equally rapidly. Her blonde hair seemed disheveled. She was thin. Fear of forgetting to take off my hat. One has to tear the hand away from the brim. Lonely, long, meaningless walk home. At such moments, the literary distance from Brod is unmistakable.

As in the previous instances of the Kaiser Panorama and the Métro, Kafka registers the mechanical music (Ariston, telephone, doorbell) precisely, as it starts up the movement, intensifying the impression of a visit to a bureaucratic office.

Kafka and Brod as Achilles and Odysseus, armed with helmets? They are more like Laurel and Hardy, attempting to make their escape from this establishment as rapidly and noiselessly as possible. As if in a photographic close-up, Kafka snaps a picture of a prostitute who is standing in his immediate vicinity. Here no space or time remains for a double exposure of the fictitious Edith and the real Fräulein Rehberger. It is like writing by the light of a flashbulb.

In the fall of 1911, Kafka and Brod make several attempts to move forward with the jointly planned novel, but it soon becomes evident that beyond good intentions and a first chapter no further "communion" (Brod) will be forthcoming. In his diary from this period, Kafka lets Fräulein Rehberger pass muster one last time, with utmost precision and a rather intrusive imagination. As if she were an acquaintance from Prague (or one of the *girls*), he concocts an erotic signal from her and lets himself be excited in a rather insidious way by her features, which are described as ugly. And once again the scene, like the "embarrassing" transfer from train to taxi at the Munich railway station, is plunged into the darkness of an artificial night. Now he can also admit without beating around the bush that during the train trip and in Munich he and Max have pursued her in a thoroughly disrespectful manner. And even more clearly than in the double exposure (Edith alias Alice/white slave girl alias Dora), Kafka now expresses his desire: "Afterward felt... several little throbs of attraction to her." On October 12, he notes: **Yesterday at Max's worked at writing the Paris journal. In the semidarkness of the Rittergasse, the plump warm Rehberger in her fall suit, whom we only** knew in her summer blouse and thin blue summer jacket, in which a girl of less than faultless appearance is ultimately worse than naked. Then we could see her rather prominent nose in the bloodless face, whose cheeks one could have pressed with one's hands for a long time before they would have showed a blush, the heavy blonde down that gathered on the cheeks and the upper lip, the railway dust that had sifted in between nose and cheek and the weak white of the throat above her neckline. Today, however, we followed her respectfully, and when I had to take my leave at the opening of a passageway before the Ferdinand Strasse on account of my unshaven and otherwise unkempt appearance (Max at that moment very handsome with black raincoat, white face, and gleam of spectacles), afterward I felt several little throbs of attraction to her. And when I reflected on why, I had to keep telling myself it was only because she was dressed so warmly.

The next day, the Fräulein Rehberger identified in this form dissolves into further "momentary observations," into individual images, not dissimilar to the precisely recollected images just a few seconds long in *The White Slave Girl*. And once again, Kafka overlays Angela (or Alice) Rehberger from the summertime train trip with that other figure he had glimpsed in the twilight of the Rittergasse. He finds the description so accurate and effective that in the process he is able to forget the person he really saw, who has been concealed—or revealed—as the "white slave girl." I did not consider the description of Fräulein Rehberger successful, but it must have been better than I believed or my impression of Fräulein Rehberger the night before last must have been so incomplete that the description equaled or even surpassed it. For as I was returning home yesterday evening, the description occurred to my mind for moments at a time, replaced the original impression unawares, and I believed I had seen Fräulein Rehberger only yesterday, and in fact without Max, so that I was preparing to tell him about her, exactly as I have described her here. `58`

Passengers view the Manhattan skyline from the harbor New York, 1939

ENTR'ACTE

He unfolds the yardstick. It is too short; he makes a mark in the air with his pencil.

Karl Valentin in the film *The Repaired Spotlight*, 1934

Between the winter of 1911 and the spring of 1912, Kafka is working on the novel *The Man Who Disappeared (Amerika)*. As he tells his future fiancée Felice Bauer in March 1913, he destroys this first version, two hundred pages in all, as "completely unusable." On May 9, 1912, he confides to his diary his desperate attempts to begin again with writing. "How I hold fast to my novel against all unease, exactly the way a figure on a monument gazes into the distance while holding fast to the base."

A month later he receives an—encouraging—echo from the nineteenth century, from his favorite writer: "Now I read in Flaubert's letters, 'My novel is the rock to which I cling and I know nothing of what is taking place in the world.'—Similar to the entry I made about myself on May 9." And in the next entry, set off by a stroke of the pen, he records the virtually physical draining that the writing has wrought in him: "Weightless, boneless, bodiless, walked the streets for two hours and thought about what I suffered while writing this afternoon."

There have been repeated speculations as to which films may have had a more or less immediate impact on Kafka's writing. He himself provides no information about this, not a single hint that he drew on certain images or scenes for his writing. The images that he fleetingly touched on and occasionally preserved—usually they are only very brief diary entries, confined for the most part to the years 1910–13—bear no immediately recognizable relation to his fiction. Indeed, one cannot escape the impression that he wanted to keep these images out of his prose, exactly as if they existed in such a provisional and fleeting aggregate that they could be described comprehensibly only in the sense of a *mimetic*, rather than an immediately *substantive* translation of their content.

The stages in the metamorphosis, or more properly, distortion of film residues into fiction are manifold in Kafka, and there is an evident and pleasurable (dis)pleasure over the fact that he is able to fix the cinematic images only provisionally and inadequately. It is gestural translation that Theodor Adorno has in mind in a 1934 letter to Walter Benjamin when he writes (with a jab at Max Brod): **Thus Brod, with his banal reference to film, seems to me to have hit on something much more accurate than he could suspect. Kafka's novels are not prompt books for the experimental theater, for they are, in principle, lacking the audience that could take part in the experiment. Rather, they are the last, disappearing textual links to silent film (which, not coincidentally, disappeared nearly simultaneously with Kafka's death). The ambiguity of the gesture is that between sinking into speechlessness (with the destruction of language) and rising up out of it in music—hence the most important set piece, in the constellation gesture-animal-music, is probably the description of the group of voicelessly music-making dogs in "Investigations of a Dog," which I would not hesitate to place on a par with Sancho Panza.**

Photography is a different matter. Here, as the example of the Kaiser Panorama demonstrated above, the "stillness of the gaze" can develop sufficiently that what has been seen can be carried over into memory and compared with already available images. Touching, no matter how often one reads it, is the scene in *The Man Who Disappeared (Amerika)* in which Karl Rossman is looking at the photograph of his parents, and when the sight of his father, even after he has contemplated it for some time, refuses to become *more alive*, turns to the image of his mother: **The mother, by contrast, was already better represented, her mouth was twisted as if someone had done her wrong and she was forcing herself to smile. It seemed to Karl that this must be so evident to anyone who looked at the picture that in the next instant it again seemed to him that the obviousness of this impression was too strong and almost preposterous. How was it possible to gain so powerfully, from a picture, the unshakable conviction of an emotion concealed by the** person who was depicted? And he averted his eyes from the picture for a little while. When he turned to look back at it again, he noticed his mother's hand, which hung down right in front from the arm of the easy chair, near enough to kiss. **64**

When Kafka has a photograph before him, he can explore and feel his way across it and enter into an almost osmotic relationship with the person whose image is represented: **This photograph, dearest, brings you a very, very great deal closer to me again. I should think it must be quite an old picture... the whole thing, by the way, the way it is lit, the placement and mood of the people who are depicted, looks quite mysterious, and the key to the mystery, which lies on the table in front next to the little box belonging to it, makes things not a whit clearer. You are smiling wistfully, or is it my mood that creates this smile for you. I may not take a proper look at you, otherwise I am unable to tear my gaze away from you... Dearest, how strong one is when it comes to pictures and how powerless in reality! I can easily imagine that the whole family steps aside and goes off, that you alone remain behind and I lean toward you across the big table, to seek your gaze, to receive it and swoon with happiness. Dearest, pictures are beautiful, pictures are something we can't do without, but they are a torture, too.** **65**

Still from *Theodor Körner* 1912

TORN AWAY,
OR LÜTZOW'S WILD CHASE

So many golden images floated 'round me,
The lovely dreams all turn to funeral dirges.
Be brave! The things that my heart holds so truly
Must live on in me there throughout the ages.

Theodor Körner, "Abschied vom Leben" (Farewell to Life), 1813

In September 1912, in the margins of a stormy entry in his diary, Kafka abruptly makes mention of a visit to the cinema. The weeks before had been filled with exciting inner and outer events. On August 13, in the Brod family home, he had met the Berlin office worker Felice Bauer—and immediately he produces, as he had earlier with Alice Rehberger, a minutely observed photographic signal that immediately takes on the solidity of a "judgment": **When I arrived at Brod's on the 13th, she was sitting at the table and yet seemed to me like a servant... Bony, empty face, which wore its emptiness openly. Bare throat. Blouse tossed over... Almost broken nose. Blonde, rather stiff unalluring hair, strong chin. As I was sitting down, I looked at her more closely for the first time, when I sat, I had already formed an immutable judgment.**

66

In November, as Kafka writes to Felice Bauer, he will introduce a new daily regimen. The schematic character of the new schedule is less surprising than the happiness he hopes to achieve by writing: **My way of life is arranged solely around writing and if it undergoes changes, then only in order to be better suited to writing, for time is short, my powers are few, the office is a horror, the apartment is noisy, and one has to try to squeeze through with tricks when it can't be done with a lovely, straightforward life... From 8 until 2 or 2:30 office, until 3 or**

A still from *Theodor Körner*. Theodor Körner (1791–1813) is the poster boy of German nationalist literature. What flowed from his pen was known as "patriotic poetry." After rebellious years at the university, in 1813, on the basis of the great success of his drama *Zriny*, Körner was named imperial playwright of the Hoftheater in Vienna. In the same year, he joined Lützow's militia, became his adjutant, and on August 26 died the very hero's death that he had glorified over and over again in his poetry.

In the *Berlinische Nachrichten* of August 21, 1813, under the rubric "Anecdotes from the Current War," it is reported that Körner had fallen victim to a "shameful" ambush of Lützow's militia near Kitzen, from which he escaped only with severe injuries. "Then, with his deep wound still unbandaged, without an evening repast, overnight he scribbled the following sonnet on his tablet, and soon thereafter fell into a mortal slumber, from which, however, he fortunately awoke to new life on the following afternoon."

There is an anecdote that is told about his childhood. Theodor Körner, who was given his first pair of trousers at the early age of three and who had been told that one of the attributes of a real man is a beard, greeted the tailor who brought the new item of clothing with enthusiasm until he noticed that there was something missing, and then asked disappointedly, "Where is the beard?"

3:30 dinner, after that sleep in bed... until 7:30, then 10 minutes exercises, naked, with open window, then an hour taking a walk... then evening meal with the family... then at 10:30... sit down to write and remain there as long as strength, desire, and happiness permit until

67

1, 2, 3 o'clock, once even until 6 in the morning.

During the night of September 23–24, on a train, he had written the short story "The Judgment" in his journal notebook and already the next morning had read it aloud to his sisters. On September 25, finally, after the furor surrounding "The Judgment," he is ready to recommence work on *Amerika*. But like Odysseus, he resists the lure of the sirens: "Forcibly prevented myself from writing." He reads "The Judgment" in his circle of friends and notes, "The indubitable character of the story is confirmed." In the evening, finally, after succumbing to writing like an addict, he can think of no other antidote than the cinematograph. **This evening tore myself away from writing. Cinematograph at the Landestheater. Box seat. Fräulein Oplatka, who was once pursued by a clergyman. She arrived home completely drenched in a cold sweat. Danzig. Körner's life. The horses. The white horse. The smoke from the gunpowder.**

68

Lützow's wild chase.

A line in ink across the page, and Karl Rossman's fate takes its course.

In the morning edition of Prague's German-language daily *Bohemia*, the following ad appeared on September 25, 1912:

German Landestheater / Popular Comedies / (Scientific cinematographic showings) / Wednesday, September 25, 1912 / Three showings: I. Showing 2:00 / II. Showing 4:30 / III. Showing 7:30 / Program: / 1. Strange Insects / 2. The Island of Ceylon / 3. Danzig / 4. In Remembrance of the Birthday of Theodor Körner: *Theodor Körner, His Life and Writing* — Early Years — the Student — the Playwright and His Bride — the Freedom Fighter.

Schedule of the German Landestheater: Saturday, September 28: V. Popular performance at reduced prices, *Eva* — Sunday, September 29: VI. Popular performance at reduced prices: *The Talisman*.

This ad, which at first glance does not appear unusual, testifies to the severe crisis that befell the theater — not only in Prague — in the years between 1911 and 1914. The best-known German-language theater, the Landestheater, also known as the Nostiz-Theater, suffered a massive decline in audience numbers due to the enormous popularity of the cinema.

Looking back at that difficult period, the chronicler of the German theaters in Prague, Richard Rosenheim, complains in 1938, in the plaintive tone of conservative cultural criticism, about the "Americanization of Central Europe":

Problem years. — Despite such peak achievements and despite the fact that the opera and the theater approached even their day-to-day work with the greatest diligence and the most profound seriousness, the years from 1911 to 1914 were difficult problem years. Those who, like the writer of these lines, were active at that time in the direction of the great theaters, know why. These were the years in which the peace of Europe was in its death throes. A tremendous tension, the premonition that something terrible was ineluctably approaching, had taken hold of the populace, and as an antidote they sought distraction and oblivion at any price. It was the era of the dance contests, the beginning of the cultural Americanization of Central Europe and, hence, the era of empty cash registers for every serious-minded theater. This was no different in Prague than in Hamburg and Berlin, in Vienna and Paris...

The awakening came too late. — For three years, Heinrich Teweles directed the German-language theater in Prague. The premiere of

Parsifal, the brilliant upbeat of the fourth year, was not a bad omen for the future. But the creeping crisis in the theater's business conditions did not allow the director to enjoy this momentary success for very long. Until now, Teweles had seen the origin of the crisis primarily in terms of difficulties resulting from the technical backwardness of the Landestheater... But the really productive utilization of the old theater remained a problem even after Teweles at last succeeded in having electric lights installed in the Landestheater. What had been a sensation in 1888 was an outmoded aperçu in 1911. Teweles, however, believed so firmly in Edison as the savior that, in his efforts to draw larger audiences to the Landestheater—the venerable theater on the Obstmarkt that had been consecrated by Mozart's genius—he came up with the odd notion of installing a *cinema*. His energy succeeded in realizing even this idea, against all resistance from above and below, and thus the first German cinema in Prague actually made its home, for several years, in the Landestheater. Naturally, Teweles adhered strictly to the guidelines that had been established when he received his permission and offered the public only culture films. But for this very reason the anticipated business success did not materialize, and a few years later, after great sacrifices for which he was only partially compensated, Teweles quietly allowed the cinema at the Landestheater to disappear again.

69

Kafka's excitedly flickering stenogram describing the opening night recalls the tumultuous nightmare of Paris. And by including the fearful episode of Fräulein Oplatka, he approaches melodrama.

Danzig has survived only in description. *Theodor Körner*, on the other hand, has been preserved as a film. *Danzig* adheres to the "strict guidelines" for enjoyable culture films that Teweles preferred. The description of the film's content reflects the bombastically pedagogical tone appropriate to a *Bildungsreise*: **Danzig. Near the mouth of the powerful Vistula River, only a few kilometers from the gulf of the Baltic Sea known as the Bay of Danzig, lies the charming city of Danzig. Once a mighty Hanseatic city, Danzig remains an important mercantile center even today, when world trade is focused more on the North Sea. Its harbor, which reaches into the center of the city, is one of the most important in the German empire. Danzig is quite remarkable in other ways, as well, especially for its architecture. If we gaze down upon the city from the tower of the splendid Gothic Rathaus, which**

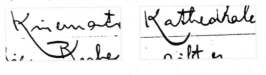

Striking calligraphic similarity between the **K** on the poster (left), above all the long outward curve of the tail at the lower right, and Kafka's own handwritten **K** (below) which he once described in his diary as his own caricature. "I find the **K**'s ugly, they almost disgust me and yet I write them, they must be very characteristic of me." Kafka, *Diary*, May 27, 1914.

stems from the 15th century, our attention, as the illustration shows, is drawn to the powerfully medieval style in which both private and the public buildings are constructed. We see numerous towerlike houses with tall, closely spaced windows and delicate, arabesquelike rooftops reaching upward; in particular, the Long Market, which lies directly below us, displays these characteristic features in purest form. Continuing our visit, we arrive next at the so-called Crane Gate, a massive Gothic structure, then at the monument to Kaiser Wilhelm I, in front of the High Gate. Evening has fallen, and we stroll down to the banks of the Mottlau River, where we admire the colorful splendor of the setting sun, which glints from the waves. As our visit draws to a close, we have an opportunity to get acquainted with the inhabitants as they go about their daily chores and conclude today's walk, which has been interesting and enjoyable in every respect, with a view of the oldest structure in Danzig, the Bakers' Workhouse.

70

In *Theodor Körner*, we have to do with a sentimental, sensational film with a perceptibly nationalistic tendency—the ad proclaims loudly that it is being shown "on the anniversary of the Battle of Sedan!!!" On August 31 of the year 1912, this is a minor sensation—with anonymous protagonists. The wild equestrian stunts are spectacular, as Kafka happily notes.

71

Albert Bassermann as Hamlet 1910

THE ARBITRARY EXAMPLE,
OR THE OTHER

Ghostly things become very familiar.

Otto Pick on Kafka's *Reflection,* **1911**

In the months that follow, no visits to the cinema are recorded—as, indeed, Kafka only writes about his cinematic experiences very sporadically and hardly ever in any systematic way.

Felice Bauer has entered less into his daily life than into a boundless correspondence with him. During the following months, she is the recipient of the most important communications concerning his abruptly vacillating impulses, his crises, his moments of happiness. Kafka makes her into the great screen onto which he projects his mostly late-night letters at a steadily accelerating pace. To her, above all, he reports on his progress and the difficulties of writing the novel *The Man Who Disappeared (Amerika)*, on the creation and first reading of "The Metamorphosis," on his enthusiasm for the Yiddish theater. "The whole Yiddish theater is lovely, last year I probably attended these performances twenty times, and the German theater perhaps not at all." Along with the magic gestural world of "dramatist" and "explainer" Jizchak Löwy and his troupe, the new cinematograph at the Landestheater held a greater attractive power for Kafka than the theater itself. The moviegoer and theater deserter confirms Herr Teweles's most tormenting fears. Always anxious, half asking for advice, half playing with this attitude, Kafka initiates Felice into all the business of his life. He is in love, quite evidently and with thoroughly conflicting emotions, and the most exciting aspect of this high-strung, panicky lovesickness may be the fact that it is possible to write so many things to the object of one's love and—with gentle pressure—expect and demand that she will respond in kind.

Hence the lasting charm and powerful irritation of these letters—we possess only his letters to her—is to be found in the fact that Kafka, without making any distinctions and with unflagging intensity, mixes (self-)doubts and hopes, large and small concerns, work, writing, and daydreams. An unbroken narrative, a "projective" claim on the attention of the other by means of significant insignificant things captivates the reader. Everything is always rooted in the writer's eloquent anxiety that he will expect too much of her while at the same time he is inevitably unable to refrain from asking even more. **I appear to myself as if I were standing in front of a barred door, behind which you live and which will never open. Only by means of knocking can one make oneself understood, and now, besides everything else, it has grown silent behind the door. But one thing I *can* do (but am I ever nervous! My inkwell has not much ink and is therefore propped against a matchbox, just now during a quick dip of the pen it slid down from the box—I, however, was jolted from head to foot and both my hands flew up in the air as if I had to beg someone for mercy), one thing I *can* do, that is: wait, no matter how much the above-parenthesized nervousness seems to contradict that. Impatience for me is just a** 74 **way to pass the time of waiting.**

After the unusually productive period in the fall of 1912, Kafka's creative powers come to an almost precipitous halt. Once, when Felice asks him about his plans and prospects, he confesses candidly and almost a little shocked, "I was astonished at the question… Naturally I have no plans at all, no prospects at all, I am not at all able to walk into the future; to fall into the future, hurl myself into the future, stumble into the future, that is what I can do and best of all I can just lie here. But plans and prospects are truthfully something I don't have, if I am feeling well, I am completely filled up with the present, if I am feeling bad, I already damn 75 the present, and how much, then, the future!" Defense in panic, says Elias 76 Canetti in regard to this very rhetorical insertion.

Hindered in his writing, in a state of only apparent rebirth, and describing this self-hindering, Kafka, fluttering anxiously, besieges Felice in Berlin with nocturnal epistles. In a paradoxical motion, he wants to push her away from him, away from his person—and for this he needs the daily exchange of letters. In a detailed allusion not only to the title of his "little story" (by which is meant "The Metamorphosis"), he portrays himself as "worthy of loathing" and "revolting": **I am a different person**

Ulrich Rauscher wrote a scathing review in the *Frankfurter Zeitung* on February 6, 1913, although its main point is an apotheosis of Bassermann's acting: **Albert Bassermann took evident pleasure in this virtuoso assignment. I cannot say that his affair with the flicks has cost him anything. The transformation of his own qualities into the "Other" was horrifyingly lifelike, not thanks to but despite Lindau. This ability to transform oneself from one human bring into another, with painful jerks and spasms, like a butterfly that has painfully freed itself from its chrysalis, is something so frightening that I have seldom seen anything in the human realm with which to compare it. The greatest part was naturally Bassermann's most personal creation—when he notices that something is not quite right about him, when every word betrays something vaguely horrific to those around him, when he feels himself hemmed in by invisible ghosts, first smiles uncertainly, becomes serious, falls silent, starts abruptly, and finally collapses like a human being who has been blasted and destroyed. There is only one god for the language of the body, on film and on the stage, and Bassermann is his prophet!**

Stills from *The Other*.

than I was in the first two months of our correspondence. It is no new metamorphosis, but a regressive transformation and probably a last-ing one. If you felt attracted to that person, you must, you must loathe the one of today… The fact that the person of today, that this person who today is so changed in every respect is attached to you unalterably and, understandably, if anything, more seriously than before, must, if you are clear about it, even intensify his revolting qualities from your point of view.

77

And in the letter of the following night he already cites what he calls "an arbitrary example" that is intended to illustrate his miserable state, suspended between *being* and *nonbeing*. The background is a stroll through the center of Prague on the evening of March 4, 1913. Kafka and his friends—among them Elsa Brod, née Taussig, to whom he had, two years earlier, so explicitly recommended two little sketches in the Orient Cinema—had paused before a cinema. The film advertised there was in many respects made to order for arousing his curiosity. On display were still photographs promoting the film *The Other*.

Kafka's closer inspection inadvertently turns into a snapshot of himself, including his entire miserable present state of mind and "distorted judgment of people": **To demonstrate this to you by means of an arbitrary example: In the lobby of the cinematograph theater, where I was this evening with Max and his wife and Weltsch (this reminds me that it is almost 2 in the morning), there hang a number of photographs from the film *The Other*. You have surely read about it, Bassermann is in it, next week it will play here, too. On one poster, where B. was depicted alone in an armchair, he seized my attention again, like that time in Berlin, and to everyone's annoyance I repeatedly dragged whomever I could find, whether Max, his wife, or Weltsch, over in front of this poster.**

Bassermann, who now seizes him again, "like that time in Berlin," was the protagonist of a noteworthy performance of *Hamlet* that took place in November 1910 in the Deutsches Theater and that enraptured Kafka—in a postcard to Brod—as much as it did the usually skeptical theatre critic Alfred Kerr.

In this *Hamlet*, Baudelaire's "chandelier" glows with particular brightness. Kerr and Kafka seem to have been equally taken with the production. Kerr writes, "All the ideas are presented with the sharpest possible clarity, the monologue 'To be or not to be,' despite the calm demeanor with which it is declaimed, is penetratingly incisive in its sharpening of the contradictions, and if the words of the script once or twice escaped the performer, the meaning emerged everywhere with such plainness that the intellectual content virtually shone out into the audience. In his [Bassermann's] interpretation, there was something inwardly experienced that communicated itself to the audience and found an echo in bursts of heartfelt applause."

"Plainness," "shone out," "inwardly experienced," "communicated itself," "echo," "bursts of...applause"—Alfred Kerr whispers the cues that Kafka picks up four weeks later and sends to his friend on Prague in a hasty postcard, enthusiastic and almost overwhelmed. "Max, I have seen a *Hamlet* performance, or better, heard Bassermann. For periods of a quarter of an hour or more, by God, I had the physiognomy of another person, from time to time I had to turn away from the stage toward an empty box to bring myself back to order."

80

In fact, in this performance Bassermann came closer to the audience than usual. "The orchestra pit was largely covered over, so that the play," as Kerr notes in his review, "could advance beyond the frame of the stage and at times unfold between the director's boxes; the part of the orchestra pit that was not covered had stairs leading down to it, over which the actors appeared and disappeared on several occasions, so they seemed to move about between the heights and the depths, between the basement and the structure rising above it, between the abyss and the heights."

Under the spell of this recollection of the Berlin *Hamlet*, Kafka approaches the still photographs that are on display and is immediately sobered: **In front of the photographs, my joy already decreased, one could see after all that it was a miserable piece in which he was appearing; the situations that were pictured were old film inventions after all, and, finally, still photographs of a horse jumping are almost always beautiful, while still photographs of a criminal human grimace, even when it is the grimace of Bassermann, can be somewhat vacuous.**

81

Kafka suggests to Felice that he is interpreting the film that is advertised based solely on the still photographs that are on display and that they enabled him to recognize the "somewhat vacuous" quality of the whole. But he fails to mention a source that has been available to him for some five weeks and that has revealed to his critical eye what he could anticipate from this film.

On January 30, *Bohemia* had carried a short piece by Albert Bassermann. In it, the actor and "established artist" summarized his thoughts on "The Actor in the Cinema and on Stage"—this was the title of the piece—on the occasion of the film *The Other* and in response to the critic Chon-Wiener. Bassermann wrote:

For the cinematic actor, the conditions of his expression are absolutely no different than for the stage actor. He has merely, if his figure is to appear in sufficient size and clarity on the white surface, to take care that he should play to the visual scope of the lens, which in this case is relatively small. Hence there are merely some minor technical means that he must acquire, for example extensive use of the eyes, somewhat more quietness in gestures, and moderation in

Felice Bauer in 1914.

the movement of the lips. Film, exactly like theater, can present real-istic or stylized dramas. But it is ridiculous to call for stylization of gestures and facial expressions as a general requirement for the cin-ema. Whoever has followed the development of cinematic acting must have remarked without too much difficulty how much more simple, natural, and, hence, effective the actors have become as soon as they are dealing with stories from life.

Certainly, the main requirement for cinematic drama is action. But since when are psychological events not action? For in the cine-ma, naturally, you cannot indulge in long reflection on some subject or other, but you can bring pain, joy, despair, woe, sorrow, depres-sion, love, etc., just as in real life. So far, Dr. Chon-Wiener seems to have seen relatively few good films—he is like a blind man talking about color. The job of the cinematic dramatist is to invent situations that are understandable with as little text as possible. Therefore, one can say that circumstances have changed for him as compared with the playwright; but for the cinematic performer this is not at all the case. He must behave exactly the same way as on the stage, while remembering the minor technical means that I mentioned above. If anything, more discretely!

82

In his instructions, Bassermann harks back to the model of the sarcastic, rhetorical instructions Hamlet gives to the three actors in the play within the play. He formulates his directives with considerably more restraint than the latter, while at the same time they are intended to satisfy two conditions that are difficult to reconcile: to act both for the small visual scope of the camera lens *and* for the stage. But Bassermann reduces the problem to "technical means," which would have to be a matter not only for the actors but also for a specifically cinematic dramaturgy, and implies that this is also applicable to *The Other*. For Kafka, perusing the still photographs in the lobby, Bassermann's cinematic performance appears "somewhat vacuous." But, surprisingly, he also "sees" that the film would be a "miserable piece." He recalls not only Bassermann's *Hamlet*, but also, as a reader who craves newspapers, the above-cited article. The article had run in *Bohemia* in the column Theater and Art right next to the very first—and most enthusiastic—review of his own book *Reflection* by the Prague journalist and lyric poet Otto Pick. At the time, Kafka had found this commentary "excessively laudatory," but actually Pick's comments were very perceptive: "This new kind of observer, as Kafka represents him unrestrainedly and hence inimitably, never sees things in themselves, nor their appearances. Concepts slip, everyday things become extraordinary, ghostly things become very familiar."

Thus Kafka's more sober response to the photographs is not, as he suggests to Felice, solely a result of direct observation, but of two recollected images from the past that now, in the lobby of the cinema, collide—the discourse on theater and cinema by Bassermann, which merely plays with Hamlet, and the *Hamlet* evening at the Deutsches Theater in Berlin, which has continued to shine across the years.

Against the foil of these images and this text, not only Bassermann's grimace but also the actor himself become "slightly vacuous." And Kafka takes Bassermann—the B. of the short piece on the actor on the screen and on stage—at his word. He follows along with Bassermann's text, in which the word "reflection" appears almost as if on cue from the adjoining column of *Bohemia*: "In the cinema, naturally, you cannot indulge in long reflection on some question or other, but you can bring pain, joy, despair, woe, sorrow, depression, love, etc., just as in real life." He peers behind these words as if behind the "little torch of the usherette in the box," in the words of Bazin, and concludes disappointedly, "So B[assermann], I said to myself, has allowed himself to be used, at least in this piece, for something that is not worthy of him"—something, in other words, that is not worthy of Kafka's *memory* of Bassermann as Hamlet. At the same time, he confesses that—exactly as Bassermann himself has claimed—"he has lived the play, after all..., has borne the excitement of the plot in his heart from beginning to end, and what such a person has experienced... is deserving of unconditional love."

But evidently Bassermann has simply translated his theatrical practice into the portrayal of "psychological action" in the film (cinematic drama), hoping, with *Hamlet* behind him, that he will be able to convince the skeptical Dr. Chon-Wiener and the dubious Dr. Kafka not only of the validity of his thesis but also of the plausibility of his cinematic acting.

We do not know how Dr. Chon-Wiener responded to Bassermann's intervention in his own defense, but we do know that, wrestling with his Bassermann memories, Kafka subjected the latter's statements to a further test, which, as it evolved, led to an even more intense self-examination. The film, which "flashes like an uncertain comet across the darkness of our waking dream" (Bazin), pursues him on his way home right up to the door of his house. **But as I was waiting downstairs for some time for the house door to be opened and looking around in the night, in recollecting those photographs I felt sorry for B., is if he were the most unfortunate of men. The self-enjoyment of acting is over, I thought to myself, the film is finished, B. himself is excluded from any influence on it, he must not necessarily even realize that he has allowed himself to be used, and yet in looking at the film he can become aware of the most extreme uselessness of the expenditure of all his great powers and—I am not exaggerating my feeling of pity— he becomes older, weak, pushed to one side in his armchair, and sinks away somewhere in the grayness of time.**

Kafka "corrects" Bassermann's attitude. He does not want either the grimace next to the shining Hamlet or the justification in *Bohemia*, masquerading as reflection, to be allowed to stand. In the theater, previously, the "self-enjoyment of acting" was rewarded triumphantly with bursts of heartfelt applause by the audience—snapshots of immediate communication between actor and public that have been made timeless by memory. Today, in front of the photographs, only the "extreme uselessness of the expenditure of effort" is revealed, which has led to nothing more than "old film inventions."

And suddenly, as if he didn't want to believe his own analysis, as if with this harsh criticism he were committing a mental sin against the revered Bassermann, he turns the entire acuteness of this insight against himself and tells the perplexed Felice that he alone should be seen as the "most unfortunate of men" and that everything he has expressed by way of reflection on the film was merely invented with respect to *The Other* and, in truth, applies only to himself. So the "arbitrary example" that he presented to Felice was only a—welcome? tactical? epistolary?—subterfuge, behind which the drama of his own misery ultimately stands revealed stripped of disguise. In describing the scenes from the film, he has saved his own emotional state until almost the very end of the letter—in a manner not very different from the procedure with the White Slave Girl alias Alice Rehberger—in order to state it then with éclat. "How false! This is exactly where the error in my judgment is to be found. Even after completion of the film Bassermann goes home as Bassermann and no one else." (Kafka, as he has already intimated, went home quite changed.) "Once he has picked himself up, he will pick himself up completely and no longer be there, but not—the way I do and would like to imagine of everyone else—constantly flutter around myself like a bird that, banished from it nest by some curse, constantly flutters around this completely empty nest and never lets it out of his sight." And at the very end, after this shocking self-accusation has been spoken, comes the last metamorphosis; as if rehearsing his own *Hamlet* tone, he says with sweet words to Ophelia, "Good night, dearest. May I kiss you, may I embrace the real body?" **87**

Ten days later, Kafka mentions that he has seen the Bassermann film, which was the object of a much critical attention. He does not contradict his first impression of the film, gleaned from the still photographs, but the visit to the cinema seems to have agreed with him and reconciled him with the once deified Bassermann. **88**

This evening, after I had slept a little and Bassermann had transformed me a little, I even felt very good at times and we—Felix [Weltsch] and I—got on well together. I could tell you a lot about Bassermann, as bad as the piece is, and however much Bassermann is misused in it and misuses himself. —Good night, love, and have a nice Sunday. I lay greetings for your papa in your eyes. **89**

Léontine Massard in *The Heartbreaker* 1913

AN INVISIBLE SIGHT,
OR THE HEARTBREAKER

Inexhaustible are the springs of genuine, deep, and pure love.

Brochure by the distributor of *The Heartbreaker*

On the night before the visit to the cinema, that is, during the night of March 13–14, Kafka writes a feckless letter to Felice, in which he expresses his faint hope that the charming correspondent in Berlin may have recovered somewhat from the suffering inflicted by his self-recriminations. And in the process, as happens over and over again, he also writes about writing.

Is she already feeling calmer? Is the suffering dissipating? After the letter of today one might think so and it would be quite all right with me, but I lack confidence. You can't read? That is no wonder: when would you have time for it? ...Dearest, how do you come up with *Uriel Acosta*? I don't know the piece either and I would imagine that I couldn't read it either, despite the fact that it is true of me what you say in jest about your brain. But perhaps such a brain has to dry up and become brittle so that in due time someone can strike fire from it. —That was what I wanted to write when my sister, I was sitting alone in the salon, rang, she had come home from the cinematograph theater and I had to go open up for her. Now I was interrupted and abandoned the letter. My sister reported on the showing or rather I asked her about it, for, even if I myself seldom go to the cinematograph theater, nevertheless I usually know almost all the weekly programs of the cinematographs by heart. My distraction, my need for entertainment drinks its fill from the posters, in front of the posters I get a respite from my habitual, most deep-seated unease, from this feeling of the eternally provisional, every time I

90

returned to the city from the summer vacations that had ultimately proved to be unsatisfying after all, I felt a craving for the posters and for the electrified tram, on which I rode home, read off the posters on the fly, in fragments, straining, as we passed them by.

He is leafing through the city. The movement of the hand is taken up by the "electrified tram" and transferred to the eyes. His hunger for images—the day before he had reported in a little note on his "accumulated craving for newspapers"—leads him to seize the posters like racing pennants as he dashes by; where he stows them, in his fund of materials, remains his secret. Only very rarely, for example in November 1915, does such a poster turn up, ghost-like, while he is half asleep.

After this mechanized stroll through Prague on the "electric," he draws a line across the page of his letter—and already he is feeling compelled, in the grip of an entirely different cinematic fantasy, to storm the fortress in Berlin—the film palace "Felice"—with his writing, which he had characterized in his letter of March 3–4 as a "knock on a barred door." He wants to storm it "like a crowd": **Sometimes, I don't know what the reason is, everything that I have to say to you presses on me especially strongly, like a crowd that wants to enter all at once through a narrow door. And I haven't told you anything and less than nothing, for what I have written in the last little while was false, not all the way to the bottom, naturally, for at bottom everything is right, but who can see through this confusion and falseness on the surface? Can you do it, dearest? No, certainly not. But let's leave that now, it is already late. My sister delayed me.** *La Broyeuse de Cœurs* **was playing, the heartbreaker.**

It is not so much that his sister delayed him; rather, he himself, through his curiosity, has filled himself so full of images and in the process evidently given his imagination such a powerful push that it has carried him far beyond the mere recording of this—quite welcome—interruption. Noteworthy is only that Kafka, who as a rule tells his correspondent in Berlin everything that has befallen him in the course of the day, does *not* tell her *what* his sister has recounted to him.

Since Kafka has elected to deny us his sister's retelling of the film, we must settle for the version of an anonymous author.

Pierre de Brézeux has everything it takes to be happy. He is engaged to a charming girl, whom he worships and who loves him. In the course of a theater rehearsal organized by the Cercle Royal,

On November 1, 1915, Kafka notes in his diary, **While half asleep saw Esther for a long time, who, with the passion that it is my impression she has for everything intellectual, had bitten into the knot of a rope and was swinging mightily back and forth in empty space like a bell-clapper (memory of a movie poster).**

We can speculate—and in regard to cinematography anything else would be inappropriate in any case—as to whether this memory of a movie poster refers to an American (or British) film ballad entitled "The Curfew Bell." The theme is taken from the ballad of the same name by Rose Hartwick Thorpe (1850–1939), who had published it in a Detroit newspaper when she will still a girl. It was drawn from the anonymous tale "Love and Loyalty" and tells of a young Englishman in America who has been arrested as a spy and condemned to death. The judgment is to be carried out during the ringing of the evening bell (curfew). His lover saves him by holding fast to the clapper of the curfew bell. "Still the maiden clung more firmly, and with trembling lips and white, / Said, to hush her heart's wild beating, 'Curfew shall not ring tonight.'"

Pierre first makes the acquaintance of Ida Bianca, famed for her titillating dance. Disturbed by the strange emotions that overwhelm him in the vicinity of this temptress, her physical forms are flawless, Pierre, in a moment of self-possession, attempts to resist the spell of her senses. But he cannot escape the maelstrom of her senses. No sooner has Ida agreed to a rendezvous than he writes to his fiancée Marthe that an urgent matter prevents him from paying her a visit. At a café table in the Bois de Boulogne, Pierre and Ida are thoroughly

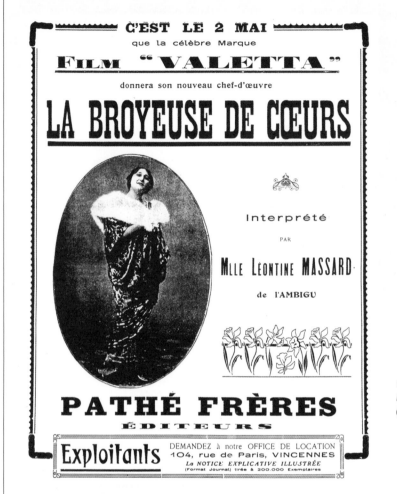

Poster for
La Broyeuse de Cœurs
(*The Heartbreaker*).

enjoying themselves. Suddenly two women stand in front of them: Marthe and her mother. Pierre blanches and blurts out some incomprehensible excuses. Marthe, her pride wounded and her heart filled with pain over Pierre's betrayal, refuses to see her fiancé. And Pierre, who in his heart of hearts still loves Marthe, becomes the plaything of the seductive Ida. Consumed with jealousy, Brézeux looks on in torment as a torero, the famous Nuovita, inundates Ida with declarations of love, and as she makes a game of driving this easy conquest to distraction—with the aim of binding her lover ever more powerfully to her. Nuovita, in the intoxication of passion, writes to Ida that he will seek his death in the bullring unless she surrenders to him. A nosegay of violets on her bosom is supposed to be the sign of hope. However, Pierre, who has intercepted the letter in Ida's absence, forgets to pass on the message, and this omission leads to the death of Nuovita. Robbed of hope, he immolates himself on the horns of the bull. Pierre and Ida are deeply shaken by this drama; in light of their inadvertent crime, they realize the brittleness of their passion. They part. Inexhaustible are the springs of genuine, deep, and pure love. Marthe, in forgiveness, does not hesitate to kiss the forehead of the one whom she has never ceased to love.

92

Following his excursion through poster-covered Prague, Kafka, who despite his evidently great excitement has told Felice only the title of the film, makes her a peculiar proposal. It enriches the intimacy of their correspondence, which has already been intensified to a level of mild terror, by a new variant that is astonishing in view of the importance that he has, for years, attached to his diary. Woven into this proposal is a "healing and edifying" justification for the significant omission, the blank space in the first half of the letter, namely his sister's retelling of the film.

For more than six months, the two have not seen each other in the flesh, but have written to each other almost daily. And then he tosses out a suggestion like bait. **How would it be, dearest, if instead of letters I would send you—pages from my diary? I miss it, not writing a diary, however little and insignificant what happens is and however insignificantly I may respond to it. But a diary with which you would not be acquainted would not be one for me. And the changes and omissions that a diary that was intended for you would have to have would certainly only be healing and edifying for me. Are you in agreement? The difference compared with the letters will be that the pages from the diary will perhaps sometimes be richer in content, but certainly always also more boring and even rougher than the letters are. But don't be too much afraid; they will not be lacking in love for you.**

93

94

"Sweet Little Things" from the operetta *The Movie Queen* 1913

THE MOVIE QUEEN

*Operetta (lat.)... In the most recent period, a burlesque or caricature opera
in which the plot is not merely witty but contains low comedy or parody
and in which the music, as well, avoids any serious emotion.*

Meyers Grosses Konversations-Lexikon, 1906

In March 1913, Kafka, who has been "transformed... a little" by Bassermann, expresses the ambivalent wish to see Felice again in Berlin—
for the first time in seven months and after having come practically
"breast to breast" through the exchange of letters. But he arranges the
preparations for the trip and the trip itself in a way that is so complicated
and confusing that after he arrives at the Askanischer Hof in Berlin he
spends at least four hours stretched out on the divan awaiting a message
from her. He had left Felice in doubt, up until the very last moment, as to
whether he would actually arrive. Finally, probably on March 24, they
manage two brief, not very satisfying encounters.

It is possible that on the evening of March 23 he pays a visit—alone—
to the operetta theater. One may see in this act, even if the visit is one
that she recommended, a kind of sympathetic exploration, as if the
"correspondent" were seeking supportive, symbolic "correspondences."

During their first encounter in September 1912, as we know from
Kafka's detailed letter a month later, Felice had told him about her visit to
the operetta *Autoliebchen* (Auto Sweetie) by Jean Gilbert. In his letter, he
virtually lets her appear as if on stage and act in front of "many
strangers"—Kafka's friends and acquaintances. Now, in Berlin, the *Kino-
Königin* (Movie Queen), by the same composer, is playing. On March 25,
the morning of his departure for Leipzig, he sends his favorite sister Ottla

83

Metropol-Theater
„DIE KINO-KÖNIGIN"

7032 2
3. Ruſka
(Delia Gill, die Kino-Königin)
Phot. Rembrandt

A postcard from *The Movie Queen*, with
Ida Russka as Delia Gill.
The back features the following poem (right).

DELIA'S ENTRANCE

I live on every corner
I stick on every wall.
In every film I may be viewed
Whatever cinema you choose!
On all the posters, everywhere,
You'll find the cinematic Duse.
They call me the eleventh muse!
Today a queen in silks and velvets
Next beggar girl in rags and tatters
Now Indian maid with fiery breast
Now Roman dame with fortune blessed
From olden days, from every side
I play women full of pride.
On horseback now, a pistol-packing
Cowgirl hunting through the pampas
I save the cattle from the pyres
Of hotly burning wild brushfires.
I chase the criminals with glee
As over steep-pitched roofs they flee.
I enter graves alive with horror
Where I'm entombed just like a nun.
And as a cheerful, happy swimmer
I dive beneath the rolling billows
To reappear a short time later
Surrounded by my cheering fellows.
I have been shot—much more than once—
Been knifed or poisoned unbeknownst
But there I am in my next film
Blowing a kiss to dear Wilhelm.
Indeed, where 'ere I stand and spring,
And love, and kiss, and dance, and sing,
O'er hill and dale, through stream and wave,
On foot, on horseback, on the train,
In submarines or in a plane,
In life, in dreams, even insane,
To catch my every word and deed
There always follow me, the flocks
Of snapping, clicking, flashbulb popping—
Photographers with cameras cocked.

a postcard of Delia Gill with a brief salutation, into which he inserts the
odd remark that he has had "no time": "Ottla, at the very last moment,
cordial greetings, don't be angry with me, I had neither time nor leisure."

96   The picture seems more important than the formulaic greeting. The
image is a message that is camouflaged by the greeting, a kind of

shibboleth, a smuggled communiqué, Kafka's riposte and response to the confidential report on the visit to the *Heartbreaker*—a sibling secret. Not a word about Felice, not a word from Felice. She remains mum—like the movie queen on the postcard.

While he was waiting in the hotel, the man who read everything, "craving newspapers," may have also come across the reviews of *Roland of Berlin*, who reports in a suggestively telegraphic style: **Spring froth in the Metropole Theater. Hurricanes of applause... At the end of the acts, enthusiastic demonstrations. The "movie queen" gazes down triumphantly from her victory chariot (drawn by Gilbert, Freund, Okon[k]owsky, the two librettists, and Schultz, the director) at her faithful followers. Hit song follows hit song. In the first act: Waltz "You Laugh, You Live, You Love"... (Ida Russka, her temperament on display from her neck to her kneecaps). In the second, "Amalia, What You've Suffered!"... (Guido Thielscher with inimitable effect on the laugh muscles. Zenith of his artistic life on earth. The public goes mad. "The people rise, the storm bursts!"...) Then the *chanson* "Sweet Little Things"... In the third, "Song of the Night"... (Josef Giampietro, smash hit, masterful performer... Salvation Army and free love, police and burglars). Fast-moving, lightly draped action, witty, prickling dialogue, glittering scenery and artful getup... Direction and staging by Richard Schultz, matched only by Max Reinhardt.**

The Movie Queen offers an ironic treatment of the hypocritical debate about movie censorship. It plays with the crisis of the theater and finally puts cinematography itself on stage.

1ST SCENE. In Berlin's Lustgarten Park, shortly after the changing of the guard, a suffragette is demonstrating. A lady is so enthusiastic about her appearance there that the suffragette invites her to her home and gives her calling card to her. The suffragette turns out to be the cinema actress Delia Gill—the demonstration was a scene in a movie. Amused, she and her director Eichwald and the cameraman Lehmann inspect the calling card of the lady, who has meanwhile disappeared. It was Auguste von Perlitz, the wife of the Minister of Culture, Rüdiger von Perlitz, married to the very man who wants to close down the cinemas because film is a sham art and a breeding ground for un-Prussian and lascivious feelings. Delia sees in the calling card a possibility to make the acquaintance of Perlitz in order to try to change his mind. She decides to accept the invitation.

2ND SCENE. Culture Minister Perlitz is sitting in a small café and giving the order to his sergeant-major Pachulke to arrest a certain Max Marder, a writer who is accused of spreading revolutionary ideas, and to bring him before the court. Auguste arrives to pick up her husband. The pair meet their daughter Anni and her fiancé, Edelhard von Edelhorst, whom the father greets suspiciously because he doesn't know anything about him.

3RD SCENE. In the Hotel Adlon, the engagement of Anni and Edelhard is about to be celebrated. Anni, her parents, and the numerous guests are waiting in vain, for the bridegroom has not arrived. Delia Gill, who is staying at the Adlon, manages with the help of the calling card to gain admittance to the engagement party, meets Perlitz, and charms him. Delia's fiancé, the actor Viktor Matthusius, who is making a film with her company, also appears. Since he was unable to change out of his costume at the film studio—the director has walked off with the key to the dressing rooms—he appears in the costume of an Hungarian Honved officer of the guard and, in a comic mood, introduces himself to the minister of culture in this guise. Since there is no bridegroom, the guests disperse. After everyone has left, Viktor wants to accompany the tearful Anni upstairs in the elevator. A short circuit brings the elevator to a halt below the second floor.

4TH SCENE. At a sausage stand, Sergeant-Major Pachulke appears with Edelhard in handcuffs. The latter has been unable to get to his own engagement party because Pachulke has unmasked him as the wanted writer, has arrested him, and is preparing to bring him before the minister of culture.

5TH SCENE. The short circuit causes a commotion among the hotel guests. Perlitz and his Auguste are horrified to see Anni and Viktor in the elevator, where they have fallen asleep. The elevator is brought back down to earth. In front of all the guests, Perlitz forces the supposed Hungarian officer to "face the consequences." He announces the engagement of his daughter and Hungarian First Lieutenant Peköffy. At this moment, Pachulke drags Edelhard, still in handcuffs, into the room and presents him to the minister as the wanted writer. Now Perlitz is happy that Anni has not become engaged to this fellow but has to accept the Hungarian officer. Delia joins them. She does not betray Viktor. The engagement party begins.

6TH SCENE. In the film studio, Viktor is acting in a scene that gives a revuelike reflection of the nightly doings in the Friedrichstrasse.

97

7TH SCENE. Delia meets Viktor in her villa. She has already almost forgiven him for his stupid prank, especially since he is developing a plan for curing the minister of his animosity to films. Delia has an idea that is even better. She has invited the minister to pay her a visit. The minister's wife has found the invitation and comes to ask Delia not to take her husband away from her. Delia promises to clear everything up to Auguste's satisfaction. Consoled, the minister's wife departs without seeing Anni and Edelhard, still in handcuffs, who have also found their way here with all their cares. As he has been instructed, Pachulke sets his prisoner free at four o'clock. Now the lovers can fall into each other's arms. They, too, leave consoled. Now Perlitz arrives. Delia has prepared everything for the performance of a seduction scene, which is supposed to be secretly filmed. Perlitz walks into the trap.

8TH SCENE. In the screening room of the Delia Film Society sit a crowd of famous guests, among them, in two boxes, the prime minister and Culture Minister Perlitz. Director Eichwald presents his latest film, *Count Porno's Last Adventure*. That's what it says, but what do the guests see? The events in Delia's boudoir—Perlitz is trying to rape Delia! The screening room is in an uproar. The prime minister dismisses Perlitz on the spot. Now Perlitz is a private citizen and gives Anni and Edelhard his blessing. That Delia has gotten the best of him is not so very unwelcome. He can finally be a human being and not just a Prussian bureaucrat.

Still from a newsreel showing the Romanov dynasty tercentenary 1913

THE LIGHT ... THE SCREEN ...
SLAVES OF GOLD

Film censorship is necessary because children need a strong hand and because
the rod is barely good enough for a classroom full of ruffians. But grownups
would do well to shake themselves free of the children more and more and avoid
any sense of belonging together with them or even appearing to do so.
Here there can be no compromise. On one side, art! On the other, films!

Kurt Tucholsky, "Forbidden Films," 1913

98

In the weeks and months following the rather uncomfortable Easter promenade through Berlin's Grunewald Park, the situation assumes an aspect of crisis for Kafka. He would like to conform at least formally to the bourgeois conventions of marriage and family, which he certainly shared, but it is precisely these high expectations that provoke his resistance, in order, ultimately, to devote himself unconditionally to literature. This dilemma, of course, lies in wait for him precisely at the point when he sees his ability to write severely inhibited. "If I could write, Felice! The desire to do so is burning me out. If only I had sufficient freedom and, above all, health for it. I believe you haven't grasped it sufficiently, that writing is my sole inner possibility of being." And in a follow-up letter the same day (April 20, 1913), he suddenly unleashes the insight "that I do not succeed even in writing in holding onto you and somehow communicating my heartbeat to you and that, therefore, I also cannot expect anything beyond writing." He introduces and inserts Felice into the chimera of a cinematic image to which he wants to hold fast like a shadow catcher, because he feels as if it is making a fool of him.

99

At the beginning of June 1913, his story "The Judgment" appears in the journal *Arkadia* with a dedication "for Fräulein Felice B." But in a letter to her he immediately adds, "Do you find any meaning, I mean, any straightforward, coherent meaning that one can follow, in 'The Judgment'? I don't find one and also cannot explain anything in it. But there is much that is noteworthy about it."

A month earlier, "The Stoker. A Fragment" had appeared in the book series Der Jüngste Tag (The Day of Judgment) of the Berlin publisher Kurt Wolff. Only a month later, this story is repeatedly and favorably reviewed, as is *Reflection*, for the second time.

But during this period Kafka, apart from rather brief letters to Kurt Wolff and a few friends in Prague, writes only to Felice. He has "written nothing for five months," he informs her at the end of June. Letter writing does not replace literary writing; rather, it is his powerful, (un)economical, and only sensible detour toward literature and away from Felice.

Great is his anxiety about entering into a really close, firm bond with her. Once he confesses to her, "only one woman, perhaps, have I really loved, so that it shattered me deep inside, that is now seven or eight years past." He encloses with this letter another letter, never sent, that he has rediscovered from "happier, unhappier times" (from fall 1912, the days that brought "The Judgment" and "Lützow's Wild Chase"). In it he had expressed in words how powerfully he saw Felice in the light of his nocturnal projections. He wanted to hold—himself—fast to her as if to an image that is moving past and moving in itself: **To hold fast: my fräulein, I interrupt my writing only at 12:30 at night in order to hold myself fast to you for a moment. I don't do it because I need it at this moment… otherwise I would not have been able to interrupt the writing. Only I am trembling all over, the way the light made the screen tremble in the earliest days of cinematography, if you remember that. I am too happy and have been suffering too much for more than a week already. I have been writing through the first half and dozing through the second half of several nights already. Days at the office and all sorts of things and my weak, miserable self. To whom to complain, if I were healthier now, other than to your great calm?** And with a last, wondering gaze at this early letter, he feels almost like Karl Rossman catching sight of the Statue of Liberty, shining in the distance: "How the sight of you affects me, even from afar!"

On July 16, 1913, after long hesitation, Kafka finally makes her a proposal of marriage. He himself, very peculiarly, speaks of a "treatise" (*Abhandlung*) in which very many more reasons are given that speak against marriage than that presage success. When he receives her "yes"—against his secret wish, as it were—he writes, "I want to marry and am so weak that my knees quake as a result of a little word on a card." And as in a bad detective movie—for example, the Nick Winter series—Dr. Juris Kafka arranges to have a Berlin detective firm gather information about his future bride—at the behest of his mother, as he emphasizes. This wounds her deeply, and as if this were not enough, he extends this destructive curiosity to her family, as well. In this "quaking" state, on July 1, three days before his thirtieth birthday, he confides the true state of his feeling to his journal far more frankly than he does to her. "The wish for unselfconscious loneliness. To be confronted only with myself. Perhaps I will have it in Riva." To Felice he writes inquiringly, arguing in an almost desperately lawyer-like way, "So in spite of everything you want to take the cross upon yourself, Felice? To try something impossible? ...I have not yet come to the end of my counter-evidence, for it is an endless series, the impossibility proves itself unrelentingly."

It is also "unselfconscious loneliness" that impels him into the cinema, just as he "tore himself away from writing" almost a year earlier in order to plunge into the cinema and surrender himself to the unselfconsciousness of a stirring film—*Theodor Körner*. In the course of this year he will plunge into the cinema several times seeking and longing for meaninglessness. He goes to the movies to forget. There is probably no more fitting place to achieve this pleasurably. And in this melancholic state he holds fast to a series of images in the literal as well as the cinematographic sense. "The honeymoon pair that emerged from the Hôtel de Saxe. In the afternoon. Dropping of the postcard into the postbox [the letter to Felice in which he tells her about the fact and the result of the spying in Berlin]. Rumpled clothing, limp gait, murky warm afternoon. Not many characteristic faces at first glance."

As if in a wipe, the image of the wedding scene in front of the Hôtel de Saxe turns into the picture (the film) of the Romanovs. It's as if the hotel guests were on their way to the tsarist celebration and Kafka were accompanying them. Everything is dipped in a tired, misty light. A feeling of sadness hangs over everything, "rumpled clothing" on the one hand, "peevish, aging princesses" on the other, "limpness" in both scenes. **The scene of the tercentenary of the Romanovs in Iaroslavl' on the Volga. The tsar, the grand duchesses standing peevishly in the sun, only one, gentle, aging, limp, leaning on her parasol, stares into space. The successor to the throne in the arms of the enormous, bareheaded Cossack. —In another scene men who have long since**

From the program of the movie company Gaumont: **The famous billionaire Richard Braxton, known as the Metal King, has set out from San Diego after traversing a good part of Middle America...** This gentleman, known for his unconventionality, is both a mighty finance magnate and an expert collector... He has not revealed to the journalists what the purpose of his trip is. He intentionally avoids his curious pursuers and all human habitation; he prefers to camp under the open sky with his companions. Illustration from *Slaves of Gold*, 1913.

106 **passed by salute from afar.**

Rapidly, Kafka holds fast to the detail that is decisive for him: the sight of the (hemophiliac) eight-year-old tsarevich in the arms of the Cossack. It is possible that the short film about the tercentenary of the Romanovs **107** was playing together with the two feature films *Fantômas* and *Slaves of* **108** *Gold*. Kafka makes no mention of *Fantômas*, but he holds fast to an image from *Slaves of Gold*, in a description that he opens up like a fan, a great

IMPRIMERIE de la Sté des ETABLISSEMENTS Gaumont PARIS. 9L 29 4

LE COLLIER VIVANT

From the unpublished memoirs of Renée Carl: Berthe Dagmar, the actress who plays Héléna, was supposed to be unable to climb to safety from the snakes that were slithering after her. Therefore it was wise to film the scene as quickly as possible, since the heat of the camera lights would probably increase the reptiles' strangling ability. In fact they wound themselves around the actress and choked her quite powerfully. Marcel, the snake tamer, finally scurried over and liberated the actress, who had not uttered a sound. It was only after several minutes that she broke down in tears. In *Gaumont. 90 ans de cinéma* (Paris, 1986), 60.

room-filling emblem. Again, as in the case of *The White Slave Girl,* he describes it in his own special onrushing language. **The millionaire in the scene in the movie *Slaves of Gold.* Hold him fast! The calm, the slow, resolute movement, when necessary the quick step, the jerking of the arm. Rich, spoiled, lulled to sleep, but how he leaps up like a serf and examines the room in the tavern in the woods where he has been imprisoned.**

`109`

A day later, Kafka notes, perhaps in an echo of an "amusing grotesque": "the fire with which, in the washroom of my sister [the real cinematic companion and secret 'movie queen'], I acted out a comical cinematographic scene. Why can't I ever do that in front of strangers?" Unfortunately, we only have the title of this grotesque, but it is already eloquent enough: *Only a Bureaucrat for a Son-in-Law*. It is hardly imaginable that Kafka, with his attraction to comic wordplay and linguistic paradoxes ("invisible sights," "larger than life-size dwarf"), would have wanted to act out or recount the "comical scene" about the bureaucratic son-in-law in front of his very serious and irony-resistant almost-fiancée Felice—much less "with fire"! In such things, the favorite sister was the preferred, indeed perhaps the only addressee. She, finally, was the one who had managed to stem the unchecked tide of written words, the urgent *Notturnos* to Felice, with her retelling of *The Heartbreaker*. And only for her, for her alone, was the lovely, bourgeois-lascivious postcard, the little shibboleth of *The Movie Queen* intended. Sole ray of light, sole pleasure in Berlin!

The "comical scene" with the Prague bureaucrat who is preparing to become a son-in-law assumes grotesque aspects when we consider that he produces this probably exonerating self-parody—in the washroom, in front of his sister—on the very evening of his thirtieth birthday (on July 3, 1913). On the following day things turn serious: **No, from now on we hold fast to each other and put our hands together properly. Do you still remember my long, bony hand with the fingers of a child and an ape? And in it you are now laying yours... Today I... told my mother at the noonday meal that I have a fiancée. She was not very surprised and responded remarkably calmly.**

And he confesses to her in this letter that his mother is asking him to have Felice's parents spied on as well. Now there is nothing amusing about this, and a month later, in another letter, he tries to make fun of the information provided by the detective bureau in a "screed, which is as horrid as it is extremely comical."

A week after this visit to the cinema, plagued by feelings of guilt and tending, in any case, toward massive self-reproach, Kafka reaches for an unusual image in order to make his situation come alive for Felice. This image also reveals why he so urgently wanted to hold fast to the imprisoned millionaire—at first only in the context of his diary. Moreover, he transforms himself into a snake, which—just as in the "collier vivant" in

Slaves of Gold, threatens the female and at the same time symbolizes his own situation, which is so contemptible and full of future unhappiness. In a convoluted way, Kafka "cites" this dual (movie) image of the millionaire imprisoned but admired for his strength and the dangerous snake. He lets this thought-provoking image shine through in his letter like a watermark, without revealing the source to its addressee: **Have I not been writhing in front of you for months like something poisonous? Am I not now here, now there? Are you not yet nauseated by the sight of me? Do you still not see that I must remain imprisoned within myself if unhappiness, yours, your unhappiness, Felice, is to be prevented? I am not a human being, I am capable of tormenting you, whom I love the most, whom I love alone among all human beings... cold-heartedly, of cold-heartedly assuming forgiveness of the torment.** `113`

First cinematograph in Verona 1907

AU REVOIR AND DÉJÀ VU

In the South, everything, I think, is possible.

Kafka

With Felice's "yes," Kafka's fears of marriage mount ominously. On July 10, 1913, Kafka writes to her, "Do you understand this, Felice, even if only from afar? I have the distinct feeling of being destroyed by marriage, by the bond, by the dissolution of this insignificant thing that I am..." In the first half of August, Felice is on vacation in Westerland on the Isle of Sylt; Kafka, although he has been requested to accompany her, does not go along.

In September, he himself departs on a rather long summer vacation. Following a two-week stay in Vienna—he where attends the International Zionist Congress and after that an event sponsored by the Arbeiter-Versicherungs-Anstalt—he continues on to Triest. From there, he travels by boat to Venice and writes to Brod and to Felice. To Brod, he mentions that he is "moving with such difficulty, and so sad," but that it is "good that I am alone." To Felice, he explains this difficulty in moving more explicitly: "Imprisoned in the hesitations with which you are familiar, I cannot move... rather, I lie flat on the ground, like an animal, whom no one (not even I) can influence either by urging or argument... It is as if I am tangled in a net; if I pull myself forward it pulls me more powerfully back again." The letter closes with a question that is answered almost automatically. "But what shall I do now, Felice? We must say good-bye."

Even more powerfully than in early July, in front of the Hôtel de Saxe,

115

116

he is now repulsed by the sight of the honeymoon pairs in front of the Grand Hôtel Sandwirth. "I crave being alone, the thought of a honeymoon inspires horror in me, every honeymoon pair, whether I imagine myself in relation to it or not, is a disgusting sight for me, and if I want to make myself nauseous I only have to imagine that I am putting my arm around a woman's waist," he writes to Max Brod two weeks later from a sanatorium in Riva.

From Venice he continues on to Verona. Seized by a great melancholy, paralyzed by his inability to make a decision, he describes to Brod the dilemma of his relationship to Felice. "I cannot live with her and I cannot live without her." And as for Felice herself, he tells her, on a postcard, **In the church St. Anastasia in Verona, where I am sitting, exhausted, in a church pew, across from a life-size marble dwarf, who, with a cheerful expression, carries a font of holy water. I am completely cut off from mail, will not receive any until the day after tomorrow in Riva, am hence as if in the other world, but otherwise here in all misery.**

It is Kafka's second meeting with the dwarf. The first was during the winter of 1911, on the trip to Friedland, in the Kaiser Panorama. The dwarf had been visible on the right-hand margin of the stereoscopic picture in which the church nave was depicted—"smooth floor of the cathedrals in front of our tongue." At that time, he had been struck by the lifelikeness of the photographed sculpture, which, in contrast to cinematography that flew by so rapidly, was imparted to the viewer: the monument to Tito Speri, the funerary statue of a widow, and this very dwarf in the church of St. Anastasia. Kafka's lasting interest in sculpture is surely also connected to the fact that in statues everything has come to rest and to the height of expressiveness, densely, compactly, and solidly. He does not need to hold them fast but can hold himself fast to them. They are a solidified, externalized symbol of his own situation. The paradoxical lifelikeness of the happy dwarf casts a sudden light on his own burden and the limits of what he is able to bear. It is almost as if this dwarf replaces the heraldic symbol of the snake in *Slaves of Gold*.

A few years later this encounter comes to his mind yet again. "Recollections of a church in Verona, where, I, utterly forsaken, entered unwillingly only under the slight duress of the duty of a travelling pleasureseeker and the weighty compulsion of a human being who was expiring from uselessness, saw a larger than life-size dwarf bowed down under

From *Arena*, September 20, 1913: *La lezione dell'abisso* (The Lesson of the Abyss). —The originality of this drama in four acts, which is showing today at the Cinema Pathé San Sebastiano, consists entirely in the extraordinary, wondrously sublime beauty of the landscapes among which it is set. It shows a genuine side of Swiss life, that cosmopolitan existence that apparently has to do only with expeditions and climbing tours and behind which lurks so many a romantic drama, so many a human tragedy. The performance is thoroughly compatible with the Alpine scenery in its rough-hewn power and grandiose charm.

a baptismal font..." The previously life-size dwarf has become bigger than life. The happy expression has disappeared under the weight (of memory).

Kafka is at a crossroads. Once again, as so often in the past. In May 1915, the dwarf reappears on last time, unnamed. The first engagement has already been dissolved. "Do not suppose, Felice, that I do not feel all the impeding considerations and cares as a nearly unbearable and revolting burden, would like most of all to throw off everything, prefer the straight path to all others… But it is impossible, once the burden has been imposed on me…"

"A fainting spell, not a postcard"—after a six-week epistolary pause, this is how he describes the depressing postcard from Verona in his letter to Felice of October 29, 1913. Another letter also testifies to this fainting spell, a note that he encloses later, like a found object, with his letter of November 6. "I am not keeping a diary at all, I cannot imagine why I should keep one, nothing happens to me that moves me profoundly. This is true even when I weep, as I did yesterday in a cinematograph theater in Verona. I am given to enjoy human relationships, not to experience them. I can verify this again and again, yesterday at a popular festival in Verona, earlier in front of the honeymoon voyagers in Venice."

Inability to experience is the self-diagnosis, but accompanied by enjoyment and craving for everything and everyone. The cinema is the catalyst for this affective displacement. One could say it is a strangely unmoved, an empty weeping that overcomes him. Nothing experienced intrudes between him and the screen. Once again, it is that "unselfconscious loneliness" that impels him into the movies, as it did just prior to his thirtieth birthday. "I am empty and meaningless in all the corners of my being, even in the feeling of my unhappiness."

On September 20, 1913, the national holiday, the Veronese daily *Arena* announces two other films along with the *Lezione dell'abisso*. We can speculate in what direction Kafka let himself drift: **Il celebro bandito Garouge (The Famous Bandit Garouge). —The reconstruction of his exploits in a three-part film entitled *The Female Avenger* can be seen today at the Cinema Edison in the Via Nuova. During the performance the orchestra will play "La Forze del Destino" and "Liebeselixir." To conclude there will be the very comical scene "Willy and the Parisian."**

Poveri Bimbi (Poor Children). —Childhood has always and everywhere had a poetic and touchingly sentimental note. The protagonists of the extended drama in three acts, which is being shown today at the Cinema Calzoni in the Via Stella, are two small but perfect actors whose odyssey will surely touch anyone who has a soft heart. The two children's suffering is the sad consequence of a love story overshadowed by the demon jealousy. It is an interesting, humanly accessible, original subject, a truly theatrical drama. —The main show is accompanied by the "Giornale Éclair" with the fashion

The rendezvous with the dwarf whom Kafka was meeting for the first time. The baptismal font in the church of St. Anastasia in Verona.

page and the most interesting news from around the world. —In the foyer we can listen to the divine voice of Commendatore Enrico Caruso thanks to the marvelous compressed air "Mirophono"—a genuine novelty!—singing the romance from *Aida* with orchestral accompaniment. The synchronization of the sound of the orchestra with the "Mirophono" is perfect.

Still from *Catastrophe at the Dock* 1913

BOUNDLESS
ENTERTAINMENT

The last time I saw him in Prague, we went to the movies, in a rather large group
of friends, I believe. In the opening program they showed street scenes from Berlin.
When the lights came back on, I thought I saw, for the fraction of a second, tears in his eyes.
"What is the matter with Kafka?" I whispered to my neighbor. "Oh, evidently difficulties
with his fiancée in Berlin again," he said. I can still see Kafka in front of me like that:
his face averted, lest one of us observe him, wiping the tears
from his eyes with the back of his hand…

Willy Haas, *Die Literarische Welt* (The Literary World)

After he has not corresponded with Felice again for six weeks, after he has not written another word and in the following months communicated with her only via a go-between, Felice's friend Grete Bloch, Kafka reinforces his decision to break off the unofficial engagement with her. It is astonishing that in the process, after talking so often about a desperate "holding fast," he refers to the separation using the identical expression that had escaped him quasi-involuntarily a few days after their first meeting in Prague, when he had written "The Judgment" in a single night and during the following night, in the midst of an intense creative onslaught, found himself "torn away from writing," and plunged into the newly-opened cinematograph at the Landestheater.

Now, more than a year and hundreds of passionate, agonizing, and tormenting epistolary pages later, he exclaims, "That I had to tear myself away, if you didn't want to repudiate me? You didn't think that? Do you not think it even now?" He tells her, without expressing it in so many words, that he will have to tear himself away from her in order to be able to hold himself fast to writing once again. "I will write again, but how many doubts have I had about my writing in the meanwhile." And in an image of "craving" without parallel, he continues, "Basically I am an

124

125

103

incapable, unknowing human being who… would be barely able to squat in a doghouse, to spring out when he is given food, and to spring back when he has wolfed it down."

The crisis of the summer culminates in meaninglessness, insensibility, emptiness. During this whole time, writing, after all, is only an intention, it is constantly anticipated and marshaled against her, the fiancée, who, in his eyes, is actually preventing it more and more. Going to the movies suggests a possible option, like prostitution. "I purposely walk through the streets where whores are." And like a distant echo from *The White Slave Girl* alias Alice Rehberger, he writes at the end of this temptation, "Not a soul would have found anything alluring in her, only I… I looked around at her twice, and she also met my gaze." This daydream is followed by a line in ink, and the diary closes with, "The uncertainty surely comes from the thoughts of F." Then, on the next day, like a reminiscence of the feelings of depression in Verona, he writes, "Was at the movies. Wept. *Lolotte*. The good pastor. The little bicycle. The reconciliation of the parents. Boundless entertainment. Before that a sad film, *Catastrophe at the Dock*, afterwards the amusing *Alone at Last*. Am completely empty and meaningless, the electric tram passing by has more living meaning."

The Danish film *Catastrophe at the Dock* is described in the program booklet as follows: **From the repertoire of the Viktoria Theater. —Now a film comes along of which we can justifiably say that it will cause quite a sensation. The Viktoria Theater is fond of the sensational, after all, and seldom has a drama been staged that is richer in violent effects than this one. Its title is *Catastrophe at the Dock*, and it takes place in a big city. The main character, an engineer, has achieved a technological triumph—the dock, which, however, due to an error in its construction, collapses on the very day of its dedication. This scene is the great sensation of the film. It was filmed last summer at the floating dock in Copenhagen, which the film company Danmark had rented, and the high point is when the water breaks in at a certain moment and carries everything along in the maelstrom. During the filming in the summer, outside on the floating dock, the water buried approximately one hundred actors and stand-ins; one nearly drowned. When the engineer sees his work destroyed, he goes mad and is brought to an asylum. Here you are witness to a very strange and harshly realistic scene that recalls *Dr. Goudron's System* at the**

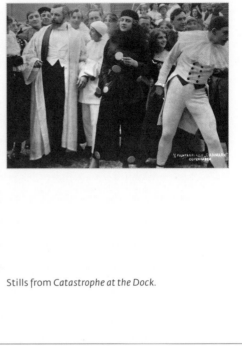

Stills from *Catastrophe at the Dock.*

Fredrieksberg Theater. Several mentally ill patients attack their doctor, but the engineer, whom they had believed was mad, rushes over and saves him, and this demonstrates that his mental state is normal. He returns home. The whole city spills over with a great carnival, and the engineer's wife is there, too. He suspects her of being unfaithful... almost collapses again, but the young woman proves her innocence, and the viewers look forward to a happy end to the numerous tribulations that have afflicted the hero. Along with serious and strange scenes, *Catastrophe at the Dock* also contains several cute ones. We could mention a tea party that takes place in the water—ladies and gentlemen in bathing suits who wade in the water up to their knees around a well-stocked table that protrudes from the waves.

Concerning the film *Isidor's Honeymoon* or *Alone at Last!*—the titles alone are an involuntary caricature of Kafka's current state—the *Roland of Berlin* has this to say on July 17, 1913: **The filming of writers and of more elevated art is progressing vigorously and has meanwhile also caught up with archcomedians Anton and Donat Herrnfeld. The**

128

Kammerspiel cinema on Potsdamer Platz considers itself fortunate to have purchased the sole rights to showings of the Herrnfeld hit *Alone at Last!* This outrageous farce, which at one time filled countless houses, is in certain respects even more effective as a film than on the stage. In any case, the honeymoon of Isidor Blumentopf [i.e., Flowerpot –TRANS.], along with the constant disturbances of his *prima nox* by the vicious cheese merchant, can be made much more visually effective in the cinema, especially since both Anton, as a hobbling hotel servant, and Donat, who is a born Isidor, have outdone themselves in their cinematic portrayals. Their gestures are so striking that you think you actually think you hear them speaking, as well. "Isn't this a lovely top hat?"—this leitmotif of Isidor, who makes use of his top hat with unbelievable virtuosity in all phases of life and decision-making, must be counted among the most effective phenomena not only of the brothers Herrnfeld but of the entire comic theater. And so one can say that with *Alone at Last!* the Kammerspiel cinema has gotten its hands on a comic hit of the first water. The writer of this gibberish signs himself "Quelqu'un."

A week later, on November 27, the diary, after an almost hopeful-sounding entry about a convalescence through writing, contains the following: "The solidity, however, that the slightest bit of writing brings about in me, is indubitable and marvelous. The look with which I surveyed everything yesterday during the walk!"—and, among a number of scattered daily observations (a sort of warm-up exercise for writing and observation), yet another recent film impression turns up. **Scene: baptism of the ships' boys on crossing the equator. The lounging around of the sailors. The ship, clambered over in all directions, high and low, offers them perches everywhere. The big sailors, who hang off the ship's ladders and press themselves with a powerful rounded shoulder, one foot in front of the other, against the body of the ship and gaze down upon the theater below.**

It is the last detailed note on cinematography altogether. Effortlessly, he binds the whole into a little garland of scenes. Again, as in the scene with the Romanovs, a young man occupies the center of his attention, but this one is strong and is getting ready to become a man. In the end, he copies himself into this image of wishful thinking—into the "big sailors" with whom he can "gaze down upon the theater below." It is an image, too, of great, longing-filled departure, this time not for Karl Rossman's new world, bur rather for a world that is altogether different—"while crossing the equator."

If, in Verona, he was depressed by the sight of the rediscovered dwarf with his immutable expression of happiness under the heavy burden of the baptismal font; here, beyond the periphery of his world—"in the South, everything is possible"—he can be the calm spectator at a male-bonding-like baptismal ceremony.

He no longer feels any compulsion to hold something, or himself, or someone else fast. He lets go of the scene, leaves the movie palace "Felice," with which, it is true, he will remain in contact throughout two more engagements and many more years; but the projection, the show-ing, the "explanations" and "treatises" (as he called the first marriage proposal) with which he freighted the heavy letters gradually wear themselves out. In 1914, an extremely productive phase in Kafka's cre- 131 ative work commences. After this scene, the next brief note on the topic does not turn up until November 1915. It is the above-mentioned "mem-ory of a movie poster." In the prose, cinematography is not thematized either as a technique or as an image; it remains oddly excluded, as if Kafka, in distinct contrast to many writers of his generation, doubted its ability to be turned into literature. That cinematic images, artfully cam-ouflaged, have entered into the slapsticklike despair of Karl Rossman, for example, cannot be automatically excluded, but the evidence for this fact, which has meanwhile assumed the status of near-certainty, is nowhere to be found.

Recovered frames from *Shivat Zion* 1921

AFTERNOON,
PALESTINE FILM

The essence of the path through the desert. A human being who takes this path
as the popular leader of his organism, with a leftover bit (more is not conceivable)
of awareness of what is happening. He has had Canaan in his nostrils his whole life long;
that he should not see this land until just before his death is difficult to believe. This final
prospect can only have the meaning of showing what an imperfect moment
human life is, imperfect because this kind of life could go on endlessly and
yet at the same time would not produce anything more than a moment.
Not because his life was too short does Moses fail to reach Canaan, but rather
because it was a human life. This end of the five books of Moses has a similarity
with the final scene of the Éducation Sentimentale.

Kafka, *Diary*, October 19, 1921

In 1921, the two engagements to Felice, the final separation from her, and his consolidation as a writer already lie far in the past. On October 23, his diary notes laconically, "Afternoon, Palestine film."

On this day, a Sunday, the film *Shivat Zion* was shown twice, in a private showing, at the Prague cinema Lido-Bio, on the initiative of the Zionist organization (and journal) *Selbstwehr* (Self-Defense). The Prague *Tagblatt* reports on Friday, October 21, under Club and Entertainment Notes: **Bar Kochba. Tomorrow, the 22nd, 8 o'clock in the evening, general meeting. A Zionist film. The Central Office of the Jewish National Fund in Prague succeeded in obtaining an original film from Palestine, *Shivat Zion* (Return to Zion), which, in a characteristic manner, shows the life of building Jewish Palestine and demonstrates the hard work of the pioneers (*chaluzim*). Along with it, the XI. Zionist Congress and Gymnastic Exhibition in Carlsbad. These films can only be seen in two showings, specifically, Lido-Bio, Havlicegasse, Sunday, the 23rd, at 8:30 in the morning and 2 o'clock in the afternoon. Ticket sale: Café Central, Lido-Bio.** `132`

The journal *Selbstwehr,* for which Kafka occasionally writes, has gone to the length of assigning two journalists to report on these films in Prague. The first one reports on the crowd waiting outside the cinema: **Outside. —"Jews in the movies!" (Židé maji Kino!)—the phrase is passed from mouth to mouth among the impatient crowd of Sunday-morning habitués of the Lido-Bio cinema, who have to wait until the Zionist film is over. "Would you believe it, now they are already even making movies!" "What an impertinence" (Ale je tó drzost), says one. The crowd is addicted to novelty only where there is a sensation or fulfillment of its own wishes, but remains fundamentally conservative. Here, in the Zionism, it detects a perhaps slight, but nevertheless characteristic, symptom of the renewal of the Jewish people, and registers amazement and displeasure. More and more salvos of applause are heard from the interior of the hall. Outside, depending on the character of the individual, the response is an exclamation of displeasure or a crude joke. "You hardly want to believe they are Jews," declares one women, who has evidently already taken a look inside, "they don't look like it at all, I don't know, but their blood must have changed!" Yes, yes—there is general agreement with her, and this is accepted as a passable theory to explain this unexpected Jewish cinema. But one fellow, a political philosopher, opines profoundly, "But it's no good" (Ale dobré te není). He obviously does not want his favorite image of ghetto Jews to be disturbed. Finally the showing is over, the hall empties—"Go back to the café" (Návrat do Kavárny), you can hear one scoffer shout—and the *Volk* can recover from the problematic of the Jewish film in the problem-free world of its own cinematic dramas.**

The second review reports on the response to the film itself: **Inside. —Meanwhile, inside, images of the new Palestine have been unreeling in front of a numerous, happily animated audience. And if, outside, there were outbursts of negative popular naiveté, inside one could be struck by an oddly positive naiveté, which dominated the Jewish film audience. They applauded the cinematic scenes warmly and stormily, they applauded Jabotinsky as he smoked cigarettes in the prison cell in Akko, they applauded Lord Churchill, Herbert Samuel, they clapped for the Jewish Legion on the march and greeted our leaders with cries of joy; even old Rabbi Meir was paid tribute in applause. The film is very skillfully and tastefully made, it brings** beautiful scenes of the new life in Palestine, in a rich alternation between city and country, festivity and daily life, politics and work. One sees the most gratifying aspect of our settlement, the new Jewish youth, girls and boys, and the most heroic one, the *chaluzim* at work and at leisure. The event demonstrated how important showings of this kind would be for our cause, how through scenes like these we come much closer to the reality of Palestine than through all the reports. It would be desirable to find a way to repeat such events as often as possible or even to make them into a regular custom. **133**

The *Prager Tagblatt* of October 21 describes the film in a similarly detailed way and in the process also mentions that the film was created "on the initiative of the English government and the 'Zionist Commission' in Palestine." The evening edition of the Prague *Presse* of October 22, also **134** provides a detailed description of the "nature shots," that is, outdoor scenes. In the Lido-Bio, the Jewish National Fund's propaganda film *Return to Zion* was shown to an invited audience. The film was produced by the firm of Bendow, in Jerusalem. This work of cinema represents neither the creation of a skilled director nor the artistry of costumed mimes but, instead, nature photography from the rediscovered 'old new country' of the new home of the Jewish people— Palestine. Neither the scenes nor the characters were scripted or posed. Better than all the proofs of the successful work of the colonizers and colonists that are given by eloquent diplomats or skilled journalists either out of sheer enthusiasm for the cause or for reasons of ambition, this sequence of scenes speaks to us with the accuracy and conviction of throbbing life. Palestine's rocky, wave- and spray-whipped coast near Akko or Jaffa, the capital Jerusalem, the Temple and the Wailing Wall, the holy Mount of Olives, Tiberias, the living symbols of the newly awakened life (I refer to the farms of the Jewish National Fund), sites from which the entire culture of the West and, one can confidently claim, of the entire world emerged, alternate with scenes from the cultural (archaeological dig at the Temple in Tiberias, with its interesting artistic monuments from the period of the Jewish empire), political (reception for the first Jewish governor, Sir Herbert Samuel, the Jewish Legion, Lord Churchill's and Naham Sokolow's speeches on the Mount of Olives), and economic renaissance of the country. These last scenes are the most fascinating ones. The streets and terraces built by Jewish workers, the planting of olive trees in Jewish earth by Jewish children, playing as they work, all these images with their picturesque colorfulness surrounded by the milieu and the richly varied population of Jews, Arabs, and Turks on the one hand, and Westerners on the other, all have such an impact on the viewer as to make the seriousness of will and reliability of deed, summed up in the constancy and lasting value of the result of both—success—believable.

The screening of this film to a private audience reflects the difficult and oppressive circumstances in which Prague's Jewish population—both the Zionists and those who felt assimilated—found themselves following the First World War. In November 1920, Prague had been the scene of anti-Semitic riots. Kafka writes to Milena Jesenská about them:

Every afternoon I am in the streets and bathe in Jew-hatred. For the first time, I have now heard Jews called a "randy race" (prašivé plemeno). Isn't it the obvious thing that one should leave a place where one is so hated (Zionism or national feeling is not even necessary)? The heroism that consists in remaining anyway is that of cockroaches, which one cannot eliminate even from the washroom.

I just looked out the window: mounted police, gendarmes with their bayonets at the ready, screaming scattering crowd and up here in the window the revolting shame of constantly living under protection.

135

The wish, which is by no means a rhetorical expression on this occasion, to leave Prague and go to Palestine, as his school friend Hugo Bergmann and others have done, runs into various difficulties. Kafka's Zionism is less visionary and less radical than that of his friends and acquaintances.

In July 1922, when he leafs through the literary history by Friedrich von der Leyen, which is organized according to "landscapes," and realizes that in a Germany that is articulated in this way there is only "German property, unsusceptible to any Jewish usurpation," the result is to make him

136

painfully and despairingly aware that he belongs to the German language and literature, rather than enabling him condemn it of his own volition. In the German language, as Kafka wrote to Brod, "the linguistic middle class" was **nothing but ashes... which can only be awakened to apparent life when hyperalive Jewish hands rummage through it... Away from Judaism, mostly with the unclear assent of the fathers (this unclarity was what was infuriating), is what most of those who began writing in German wanted, they wanted it, but with their back** legs they still stuck fast to the Judaism of the father and with their front legs they found no new ground. The despair over this was their inspiration. For the Zionists, the "new ground" was no longer to be found in German-speaking territory. For them, the coming realm was called the "old new country," as the founding father of Zionism, Theodor Herzl, called it in a reference to the oldest Prague synagogue.

In an ecstatic and anxiety-filled letter, Kafka describes and underscores his existence as a writer, which is established as an absolute, and names the lifelong price that will have to be paid for it. The external occasion for the letter is his anxiety about a little trip. What I played at will really happen. I have not bought myself free of it by writing. My whole life long I have been dead and now I will really die. My life was sweeter than that of the others, and now my death will be all the more terrible. The writer in me will naturally die immediately, for such a figure has no ground, no permanency, is not even dust... I have remained clay, I have not made the spark into a fire, but used it to illuminate my corpse.

"No ground, no permanency, ...not even dust." The writer who pulls the ground out from under himself with such radicality can no longer really emigrate, he is always already isolated in multiple ways and in a certain sense also exiled—as a writer, a bachelor, and a Jew. "I left home and must constantly write home, even if all home should have long since drifted away into eternity. This entire writing is nothing but Robinson's flag on the highest point of the island."

How seriously he pursued his own intention of going to Palestine is something that is difficult to ascertain today. But it is impossible not to hear, over and over again, the tone of unadulterated longing *and* resignation. Writing to his sister Valli, he calls the emigration of an old Jewish acquaintance, "something monstrous, to take his family on his back and carry it through the sea to Palestine. That so many of his type do this is no less great a miracle from the sea than the one among the reeds."

And in December 1921, he describes in detail for his friend Robert Klopstock how attractive Palestine must be for doctors. For his own trade—here Kafka revealingly means lawyers and not writers—his prognosis is less optimistic. It is striking that in this context he again evokes the image of dust and earth. The clay, out of which he conceives the writer (like the golem) to have been made is closely linked to this complex of metaphors. The choice of a profession—that you should have become something other than a doctor is something that has never occurred to me since I have known you even slightly. That this is an occupation for wealthy people is probably true for Central Europe, but for the rest of the world and especially for Palestine, which begins to enter your field of vision so fortuitously, not so. And after all, it is a physical occupation too. And then, too, the half-and-half professions, i.e., professions without serious grounds, are disgusting, whether they are physical or mental, but when they are concerned with human beings they become magnificent, whether they are physical or mental. This is terribly simple to recognize and it is terribly difficult to find the living path through it. For you, by the by, it is not even so difficult, for you are a doctor. In the main it applies to the mediocre mass of lawyers, that they must first be ground into dust before they are allowed to go to Palestine, for Palestine needs earth, but not barristers. There is an inhabitant of Prague with whom I am slightly acquainted, who after a few years studying the law gave it up and became a plumber's apprentice (simultaneously with his change of profession he married and already has a young son), has now almost completed his apprenticeship and in the spring is going to Palestine.

142

In the spring of 1923, already deeply marked by disease, he writes from Berlin, where he is living with Dora Diamant, to his sister Ottla, looking back: I saw that if I somehow wanted to go on living I would have to do something very radical, and wanted to go to Palestine. I would certainly not have been capable of doing so, am also rather unprepared in Hebrew and other respects, but I had to give myself some kind of hope. (With regard to Palestine it should be added that it was also chosen on account of the lungs, and also on account of the relatively inexpensive cost of living, since I would have stayed with friends. Inexpensiveness and costs are something that should be talked about more often in general, in keeping with the truth.

143

Berlin was to become his provisional Palestine. Dora Diamant, the Eastern Jew who can recite Isaiah for him in Hebrew, becomes the companion of the last year of his life. In a letter to Milena, be compares Berlin explicitly with Palestine. "I started to think of the possibility of moving to Berlin. This possibility was not much stronger, at that time, than the possibility of Palestine, then it became stronger after all."

144

A few days after the commentless film note of October 23, 1921, Kafka portrays himself in the diary as the viewer of a family "film" in which images of Palestine flicker with longing. He accuses himself of not having truly swum away, or emigrated, and, instead, of having settled for "postscripts" that have finally gained the upper hand as illustrations of meaninglessness, of an unlived life. **My parents were playing cards; I sat there alone, an utter stranger; my father said I should play, too, or at least look on; I made some excuse or other. What did this refusal, repeated many times since childhood, mean? …I am, to judge by this, in the wrong when I complain that the river of life has never swept me up, that I never got away from Prague, never was pushed in the direction of sport or craft, etc. I would probably always have rejected the offer, just like the invitation to the game. Only what was meaningless was allowed in, the study of law, the office, then later senseless postscripts, like a bit of work in the garden, woodworking, and so on.** 145

And in the entry that follows it, dated October 29, he names the only country in which he feels at home, the "borderland," his own personal *Altneuland:* "On one of the next evenings I really did take part, by jotting down the results for Mother. But it did not result in being closer, and even if a trace of that was present it was overcome by fatigue, boredom, mourning for the lost time. This borderland between loneliness and company I have only very rarely gone beyond, I have even made myself more at home there than in loneliness itself. What a lively, lovely country, in comparison, was Robinson's island." 146

Palestine remains for Kafka an unreachable terrain, a ground he is unable to tread, near enough to touch and far away—an imaginary space, a film.

Still from *Modern Times* Charlie Chaplin, 1936

POSTSCRIPT

To go to the movies is to approach oblivion, driven by the hope of transformation.
No one goes to the movies to become more sensitive, experienced, and cultivated, even if
he thinks he does. Everyone wants to be swept into the land of an inexorable miracle. He enters
the still undarkened space of the cinema like the site of a reliably occurring excess.

Frank Böckelmann, *Ins Kino* (To the Movies), 1994

In the middle of January 1923 — Kafka is living in Berlin-Steglitz with Dora Diamant in extremely modest material circumstances — he writes a note in Czech on the back of a letter to his sister Elli in Prague. The note is addressed to Fräulein Werner, the household helper of the family. **Saturday I am expecting a visitor, Fräulein Bugsch from Dresden is coming with her girlfriend the performance artist, who is going to present an evening here. If I were to go to it, it would be the first evening here in Berlin that I was out of the house, I am a complete indoor animal. I know nothing even about the cinema, here you don't learn much that is new anyway, Berlin was poor for so long, only now could it buy itself *The Kid*. For months it has been playing here...** 147

NOTES

1 [P.i] Prague's compass was magnetically oriented to Paris. With the needle oscillating between France and Germany, and above all between Paris and Berlin, the object was to find the current that would make it possible to be or become *absolutely modern*. Among the numerous establishments that opened before 1914, the Bio Lucerna deserves special mention. Located in a passage between the Wenzelsplatz and the Wassergasse, it was connected to a cabaret and a café and was the most elegant [of the cinemas]. It is still in operation today.

2 [P.v] "Omnia Pathé... So here we stood at the source of so many of our enjoyments, once more at the center of a business whose rays shone so powerfully over the whole world that one would almost rather not believe in the existence of a center . . ." From *Max Brod, Franz Kafka: Eine Freundschaft*, 1: 209f.

3 [P.8] Under his pseudonym Nino Frank, Henri Clouzot reported on the short film that launched cinematography, *The Arrival of a Train at the Station of La Ciotat*, by the Lumière brothers. **The train appears on the horizon. We can clearly see the locomotive, which grows in our field of vision, appears before us with lightning speed, and comes to a halt right in front of the station.** From Henri Cluzot, "Le cinéma en 1896," *Pour Vous* (July 10, 1930).

↓

4 [P.9] Kafka, letter to Max Brod, August 22, 1908. In this letter, Kafka is probably referring to the great Prague Jubilee Exposition for Industry and Trade, which, among other things, featured "showings of scenes from cinematographic advertisements on the wall in front of the Bioskop Pavilion." It is possible that during his visit to this exposition he purchased the postcard that he sent two years later from Prague to Max and Otto Brod in Paris. The tiny Japanese characters on the side of the top card (left, "postcard," and right, "Photostudio *** Tokyo") support this assumption. Thanks to Tomoko Takemura of Tokyo for deciphering the text. The postcards are shown below.

↓

5 [P.9] [*Arbeitsheft*: literally "workbook"–TRANS.] Kafka will not speak of a diary, in an emphatic sense, until the end of 1910. It is now assumed that the first entries should be dated spring 1909.

6 [P.9] On the history of the railroad, see Wolfgang Schivelbusch, *Geschichte der Eisenbahnreise: Zur Industrialisierung von Raum und Zeit im 19. Jahrhundert* (History of Railroad Travel: On the History of the Industrialization of Space and Time in the 19th Century; Frankfurt am Main, 1977), chapters 8 and 9.

7 [P.10] [Rudolf Kassner (1873–1959), Austrian philosopher and critic –*trans.*] Kassner wrote on Nietzsche, among other subjects. Toward the end of his studies, Kafka was interested in Kassner especially on account of his investigations into the psychological nature of various human phenomena.

8 [P.10] Kafka to Max Brod, December 15, 1908, in *Max Brod, Franz Kafka: Eine Freundschaft*, 2 vols., ed. Malcolm Pasley (Frankfurt am Main, 1987–89), 2: 50.

9 [P.13] This poster (right) advertises *The Gallant Guardsman*, another film of Pathé Frères:

Drinking and gambling, two French guardsmen are admiring a graceful young gypsy who is dancing for them. One of the soldiers gets up and whispers something in the young woman's ear, whereupon she smiles at him, and the two young people go off arm in arm, leaving the others.

Two tramps have also observed the scene. They sneak after the pair and assault the soldier. But the soldier defends himself and kills one of his attackers. The other tramp runs to a passing policeman and accuses the soldier of murdering his friend. The guardsman is court-martialed and condemned to death. The gypsy sees her friend being led away; she forces her way into the court and tells the judge about the drama that has been played out on her account. The judge now orders the release of the condemned man, and the gypsy arrives at the town square just in time to prevent his execution.

The advertisement's clumsy language is almost a mimetic reproduction of the film's crude dramaturgy. Here one might speak unhesitatingly of a "mirroring" of one medium in the other. As might have been expected, the effort to purify the "primitive" movies extended to the language in which the films were described. It could only be pleasing to the exorcists of language that as a result of this purism a lovely literary bastard— the genuine product of a "low culture" that was nearly established—had scarcely seen the light of day before it vanished again.

↓

Pathé frères, Kinematographen und Films, Berlin W. 8
Friedrichstr. 191. Eingang Kronenstr. 14.

8. Serie.

Dramatische und realistische Szenen.

2543
Telegr.-Code: *Foliole.*

Der galante Gardist.

Länge 175 m.   Preis Mk. 175.—

(Preiserhöhung für Virage Mk. 15.—).

Beim Trinken und Spielen bewundern Französische Gardisten eine anmutige, junge Zigeunerin, die für sie tanzt.

Der eine der Soldaten erhebt sich und flüstert dem jungen Mädchen etwas ins Ohr, worauf letztere ihn lächelnd ansieht, und beide junge Leute entfernen sich von den anderen Arm in Arm.

Zwei Strolche haben den Vorgang beobachtet; sie schleichen hinter dem Paare her und überfallen den Soldaten. Dieser wehrt sich jedoch und tötet einen seiner Angreifer. Der andere Strolch eilt zur Patrouille und klagt den Soldaten an, seinen Freund ermordet zu haben.

Der Gardist wird vor ein Kriegsgericht gestellt und zum Tode verurteilt. Die Zigeunerin sieht wie ihr Freund abgeführt wird; sie verschafft sich gewaltsamen Zutritt zum Gericht und erklärt dem Richter das Drama, das sich ihretwegen abgespielt hat. Der Richter verfügt nunmehr die Freilassung des Verurteilten, und die Zigeunerin kommt gerade noch rechtzeitig auf dem Platze an um die Exekution zu verhindern.

Man verlange Buntdruckplakate 120×160
pro Stück 0,50 Mk.

10 [P.13] Kafka to Elsa Taussig, December 28, 1908, in *Max Brod, Franz Kafka: Eine Freundschaft*, 2: 50ff.

11 [P.15] Rudolf Borchardt, letter to Philipp Borchardt, summer 1898, in *Rudolf Borchardt, Briefe, 1895–1906*, vol. 2 of *Gesammelte Briefe*, ed. G. Schuster (Munich, 1995).

12 [P.16] Ulrich Rauscher, "Die Welt im Kino" (The World in the Cinema), *Frankfurter Zeiting*, December 31, 1912, reprinted in *Kein Tag ohne Kino: Schriftsteller über den Stummfilm* (Not a Day without Cinema: Writers on the Silent Film), ed. Fritz Güttinger (Frankfurt am Main, 1984), 135f.

13 [P.16] Kurt Pinthus, ed., *Das Kinobuch* (1913–14; reprint, Zurich, 1963).

14 [P.17] Franz Kafka, "The Aeroplanes at Brescia," in *Max Brod, Franz Kafka: Eine Freundschaft*, 1: 24ff.

15 [P.18] The back of this postcard is shown below.
↓

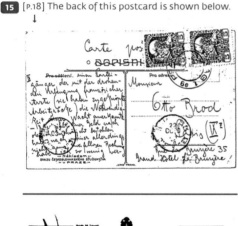

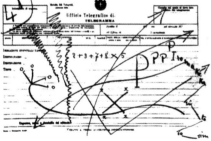

16 [P.20] In 1908, Jean Metzinger exhibits the first "cubist" paintings in the Gallery Uhde in Paris. Brod probably saw these pictures there. The critic Roger Allard comprehends and publicizes the essence of the new art in October 1910, even earlier than Apollinaire. His characterization helps us recognize Kafka's postcard series as a cubist parallel text. Invisible correspondences relate to visible correspondences. Allard writes: **In reality a painting by Metzinger strives to summarize the entire three-dimensional multiplicity of an aspect, and nothing else. In this way, in contrast to impressionism, an art is born that does not hesitate to copy details that are sometimes trivial but that offers to the viewer's understanding the essential elements, in all their painterly richness, of a synthesis that is anchored in the passing of time.** Six months later, in April 1911, this "synthesis" is given a decisive technical turn by Apollinaire: **The cinematographic art, in several ways, has the aim of showing us sculptural truth in all its aspects, without letting them fall for the benefit of perspective.** In the same year, Marcel Duchamp goes a step further with his panel painting in the spirit of Muybridge, *Jeune homme triste dans un train*. Kafka no longer wants to see his travel impressions framed by an established genre or edifying perspective. But he will not succeed in fully manifesting the credo of his cross-readings—*je vois tout / je suis partout*—until the second Paris voyage in 1911. See Fritz Metzinger, Daniel Robbins, and Jean Metzinger, *Die Entstehung des Kubismus: Eine Neubewertung* (The Origins of Cubism. A Reevaluation; Frankfurt: 1990); Guillaume Apollinaire, *Die Maler des Kubismus* (The Painters of Cubism; Zurich, 1956); Thierry de Duve, *Pikturaler Nominalismus. Marcel Duchamp. Die Malerei und die Moderne* (Pictorial Nominalism. Marcel Duchamp. Painting and Modernism; Munich, 1987). Reproduced to the left is Marinetti's *Telegramma 69* (1914–15).
←

17 [P.21] For Franz Hessel's *flaneur*, Berlin remains a text that is difficult to describe but nonetheless legible: **To be a *flaneur* is to conduct a reading of the city in which human faces, displays, shop windows, café-terraces, streets, automobiles, trees become nothing but letters with equal rights, which together make up the words, sentences, and pages of a new book.** In contrast, Kafka's nightmarish late-night perambulations through Paris seem like a painful palimpsest that has been applied to his own skin and is now scarcely decipherable. Franz Hessel, *Spazieren in Berlin* (Leipzig and Vienna, 1929), reprinted in *Sämtliche Werke in fünf Bänden. 3. Städte und Portraits* (Oldenburg, 1999), 103.

18 [P.21] Strange coincidence of perception and representation: in 1907, Windsor McCay, in his cartoon "Dream of the Rarebit Fiend," draws a figure with abscesses of ink that multiply with each successive frame until in the final frame they are erased and the figure wakes up spotless. The cartoon is below.

↓

19 [P.22] Kafka to Max and Otto Brod, October 20, 1910, in *Max Brod, Franz Kafka: Eine Freundschaft,* 2: 80f.

20 [P.23] On cross-reading, see Karl Riha, *Cross-Reading and Cross-Talking: Zitat-Collagen als poetische und satirische Technik* (Cross-Reading and Cross-Talking: Collages of Quotations as Poetic and Satirical Technique; Stuttgart, 1971).

21 [P.23] On January 10, 1775, Lichtenberg writes from London to Baldinger in Göttingen: **I would like to paint you a fleeting picture of an evening in London in the street, which I will not only paint in words but fill in with several groups that one would rather not sketch in such a permanent medium as ink... To the unaccustomed eye, all this seems like magic— one must take all the more care to watch everything attentively; for the moment you stand still—bump! a delivery boy runs into you and cries out "By your leave" when you are already lying on the ground. In the middle of the street are carriage after carriage, lorry after lorry, and cart after cart. Through this din, and the buzzing and clatter of thousands of tongues and feet, you hear the ringing of church towers, the bells of the postal employees, the organs, fiddles, accordions, and tambourins of English Savoyards, and the shouts of the people who are hawking cold and hot food on the corners of the street in the open air... In between you might hear the occasional cry of a hundred people calling out at once, as if a fire were breaking out or a building collapsing... Where it widens, everyone runs, no one looks as if he were going for a walk or looking on; rather, they all seem to be called to the bedside of someone who is at death's doorstep. That is Cheapside and Fleet Street on a December evening.** *Schriften und Briefe* (Writings and Letters), ed. Wolfgang Promies (Munich, 1967), 4: 210 ff.

22 [P.23] In his repeated use of the word "Pflaster," which means both pavement and poultice, Kafka may be delicately suggesting an anxiety about syphilis. –TRANS.

23 [P.25] From *Die Briefe des Michelagniolo Buonarroti,* trans. Karl Frey (Berlin, 1907), 206, no. 116.

24 [P.25] The Ariston is a mechanical music machine, a so-called "salon organ" with circular discs of cardboard that have been perforated; it is played by turning a crank. An Ariston from *The Kaiser's Names* (1910) is shown below.
↓

25 [P.26] *Franz Kafka: Reisetagebücher in der Fassung der Handschrift* (Frankfurt am Main, 1994), 15 f. A fascimile of this journal entry appears below.
↓

26 [P.26] In this French neologism, *feuille* (leaf) and *feuilleter* (to leaf) are contaminated with *voletter* (to flap). I am indebted for this insight to a note by Klaus Englert to his translation of Gilles Deleuze, *Das Zeit-Bild* (L'image-temps), Kino, no. 2 (Frankfurt am Main, 1991).

27 [P.26] *Was ist das Kino?* translation of *Qu'est-ce que le cinéma. II. Le cinéma et les autres arts* (Paris, 1959), 101. Kafka's reaction to a *Hamlet* performance with Bassermann (see P.74) describes precisely this radiance of the theater.

28 [P.26] Hugo Bergmann, a schoolmate of Kafka's, has given us an astonishing example of this occasionally obsessive mnemonic technique. I remember, one time we were walking by the shop window of a big bookstore (in the Minuta Building next to the Rathaus; the bookseller was named Storch). Suddenly Franz said to me, "Test me. We will go to the shop window, I will close my eyes, you tell me titles of books, and I will guess the names of the authors." And he succeeded. In *Universitas* 27 (1972): 742.

29 [P.28] "A hunchbacked but happy little man"— The author refers to Walter Benjamin's famous short sketch "Das bucklicht' Männlein" (The Little Hunchback), which appears in his book of reminiscences *Berliner Kindheit um Neunzehnhundert* (Berlin Childhood circa Nineteen Hundred). "The Little Hunchback" contains an explicit reference to early cinema: I imagine that that "whole life," of which it is said that it passes before the eye of a dying man, is composed of such images as the little hunchback has of all of us. They flit rapidly by like those pages in the tightly bound little books that were once the precursors of our cinematographs. With slight pressure, the thumb moved along their cut surface; then for seconds at a time images became visible that scarcely differed from one another. In their fleeting passage they made it possible to recognize the boxer at work and the swimmer as he struggled with the waves. The little hunchback has images of me, as well... Walter Benjamin, *Gesammelte Schriften*, vol. 4, pt. 1 (Frankfurt am Main, 1991), 302–4. The same volume contains a sketch titled "The Kaiser Panorama." –TRANS.

30 [P.29] The term Zischler uses is "Leporello," which refers to an accordion-folded album of photographs or printed images. The term apparently derives from the scene in *Don Giovanni* where Leporello regales the don and the audience with an accounting of his many loves. –TRANS.

31 [P.33] *Max Brod, Franz Kafka: Eine Freundschaft*, 2: 90.

32 [P.33] The Danish title was *Den Hvide Slavehandels sidst offer*. The film ran in English under the title *In the Hands of Imposters*.

33 [P.34] Samples of this kind of ephemera—in this case, newspaper advertisements for showings of *The White Slave Girl*—are shown below.
↓

34 [P.35] *Max Brod, Franz Kafka: Eine Freundschaft*, 2: 173 ff. The sound of this sentence in German creates a quasi-magical link between the German "**K**ellersperspekitve," the name **K**afka, and his character **K**—a link that also extends to the German word for cinematograph, **K**inematograph.

35 [P.35] Kafka, from "Reise Lugano—Mailand—Paris—Erlenbach" (1911), in *Max Brod, Franz Kafka: Eine Freundschaft*, 1: 144.

---

36 [P.37] Max Brod and Franz Kafka, "Erstes Kapitel des Buches 'Richard und Samuel,'" in *Max Brod, Franz Kafka: Eine Freundschaft*, 1: 196 ff.

---

37 [P.38] Brod and Kafka, "Erstes Kapitel," in *Max Brod, Franz Kafka: Eine Freundschaft*, 1: 198.

---

38 [P.38] Mrs. Marguerite Engberg, of Copenhagen, who was most helpful to me during my research in Danish archives, was able, in 1991, to provide a colorization of this film that was true to the original. In his book *Kafkas Roman Der Verschollene ("Amerika")* (Stuttgart, 1965), Wolfgang Jahn erroneously describes and analyzes another version of *The White Slave Girl*, in which the scene that Kafka described so accurately does not appear at all.

It is surely no accident that *The White Slave Girl, Part 2*, set the standard for a genre that at the time was virtually waiting to be invented: film criticism. Apart from brief, aphoristic, or very general comments, it was not customary, until 1911, to review an individual film, especially if it was one of the so-called trashy variety. On March 3, 1911, Czech writer Jiří Mahen published an unusually extensive critique of this film in the newspaper *Lidove Noviny*. It was the opening salvo of (Czech) film criticism: **I went there, and, indeed! The place sold out, crowds everywhere. And everywhere, the strange vibrations that you always feel whenever it is about something ticklish. The women do not look at all self-confident, the men are in a hurry, and outside stand young fellows, who, for the tenth time already, are conspiring to get in. And then the bell rings and the most sensational contemporary drama, which was produced at the behest of the Association to Oppose Trafficking in Women, begins. Fräulein Edith has become an orphan and is travelling to London to relatives. At the railway station a lady approaches her and offers her assistance for the remainder of the voyage. Edith accepts with pleasure and departs. The lady, however,** is a decoy for the slave-trader who traffics in young girls—"these beasts and bandits of human society"—and she succeeds in luring Edith into the bordello. This occurs with the help of very clever telegrams, and Edith falls unsuspectingly into the hands of a madam, a bordello mother. In the bawdy house of the madam, two young gentleman immediately fall in love with her and compete to ravish her. A wealthy lord wants to kidnap her, but an even wealthier debauchee prevents this, attacks the lord, and kidnaps Edith, taking her to his house. We have just gotten to the best part when the intermission comes. The film, of which there is already approximately a kilometer, is re-wound. And then we fly on. The debauchee wants to overpower Edith, but Edith defends herself. Some Creole woman makes the desperate girl suffer hunger pangs. But meanwhile, some engineer who has already fallen in love with the girl while she was on the ship is working on behalf of the unfortunate victim. He discovers where Edith is, wants to kidnap her in an automobile, but is ambushed again by the lord's thugs, who drag the girl off to an ordinary whorehouse. And now everything suddenly proceeds like clockwork. The police get involved, cars chase each other back and forth, shootouts above the rooftops, and finally Edith is naturally rescued and throws herself into the arms of her lover and husband-to-be. And anyone who has a conscience in his breast and reason in his head just about has to vomit... It is a perfectly ordinary cinematographic stupidity, nothing more. *The White Slave Girl*—that would have to be a different film altogether—and a kilometer of it would not be enough! And it would have to be neither moralizing claptrap nor a mere tract in favor of naked sensuality. Peter Alterberg has understood this very well.**

Mahen has inadvertently strayed from the arena of film criticism and anticipates his own sound film. **The real tragedy of white slavery is something one could capture better with sound, with soul and heart, rather than with light and reason. There you have the rustle of the new clothes in which Edith, the girl from the country, goes among the guests for the first time, and the sound of the hesitant steps** in the room upstairs when the first, extremely strange night is almost over and the new girl finally, finally can go to sleep alone!

The explicit reference to Viennese coffeehouse poet Peter Altenberg is perhaps the most surprising leap in this critique, the more so since Altenberg was an unabashed apologist for kitsch movies and, from this point of view, should certainly not have been cited by Mahen. Altenberg, whom Kafka once characterized as a "genius of trivialities," wrote in 1912, **I herewith cast my vote to ostracize all those who have recently been turning against the movie theaters, with "the best of intentions" or out of business interest! It is the best, simplest education and takes your mind off your boring ego... In the cinema, I experience the world... The people should rise up for the movie theaters and not let themselves be tricked and seduced, recently, in the littlest and most irrelevant things, by the "psychological clowns" of literature! My tender 15-year-old girlfriend and I, a 52-year-old, cried hot tears over the nature sketch _Under the Starry Sky_, in which a poor French canal boat-hauler pulls his dead fiancée upstream, slowly and with difficulty, through blooming fields... A "famous author" said to me, "We are now alone together, so tell me, what do you actually find so special about the moving picture shows?!?" "No," I said, "we are not alone together; you are alone beneath me!"** Peter Altenberg, in _Wiener Allgemeine Zeitung_, April 1912, reprinted in _Kein Tag ohne Kino_, 63 f.

[Altenberg's joke is a pun based on the fact that the German expression for being alone with someone, "unter sich sein," literally means to be under one another. –TRANS.]

39 [P.41] Brod and Kafka, "Erstes Kapitel," in _Max Brod, Franz Kafka: Eine Freundschaft_, 1: 199.

40 [P.41] Brod and Kafka, "Erstes Kapitel," in _Max Brod, Franz Kafka: Eine Freundschaft_, 1: 199 f.

41 [P.42] Brod and Kafka, "Erstes Kapitel," in _Max Brod, Franz Kafka: Eine Freundschaft_, 1: 200.

42 [P.44] "What should never have happened has happened," writes _La Domenica del Corriere_. Of all people, it was a painter—Orland Campbell—who discovered that the painting was missing. When he asked where the _Mona Lisa_ was, he was told by the guard, "She is probably in the photography studio." The full front page of _La Domenica del Corriere_ is shown below.
↓

43 [P.46] Kafka, "Reise Lugano—Mailand—Paris—Erlenbach," in _Max Brod, Franz Kafka: Eine Freundschaft_, 1: 160.

44 [P.46] The Teatro Fossati, so called after its founder, Carlo Fossati, was inaugurated while the Habsburgs were still in power, in April 1857. It was located near the former Porta Comasina, now the Corso Garibaldi. It was a popular theater, and until well into the 1920s, when it was transformed into a cinema, it was the place where the most important plays and actors of Lombardy were presented to the public. See the extensive monograph by Lamberto Sanguinetti, *Il Teatro Fossati di Milano* (Milan, 1972). The interior of the theater is shown below.
↓

45 [P.46] Kafka, "Reise Lugano—Mailand—Paris—Erlenbach" in *Max Brod, Franz Kafka: Eine Freundschaft*, 1: 157.

46 [P.46] A photograph of Edoardo Ferravilla (in costume) is shown below.
↓

47 [P.46] Kafka, *Reisetagebücher*, Sept. 5, 1911.

48 [P.47] Kafka, "Reise Lugano—Mailand—Paris—Erlenbach" in *Max Brod, Franz Kafka: Eine Freundschaft*, 1: 164.

49 [P.47] A poster from the Omnia Pathé theater is shown below.
↓

50 [P.49] Max Brod, "Kinomatograph in Paris," in *Max Brod, Franz Kafka: Eine Freundschaft*, 1: 209 f.

51 [P.49] A still from *Nick Winter and the Theft of the Mona Lisa* is shown below. Croumolle is in bed.
↓

52 [P.51] Brod, "Kinomatograph in Paris," in *Max Brod, Franz Kafka: Eine Freundschaft*, 1: 212 f.

53 [P.51] Brod, "Kinomatograph in Paris," in *Max Brod, Franz Kafka: Eine Freundschaft*, 1: 211 ff.

54 [P.52] It is more than a curiosity to recall that the two occasionally preferred to speak Czech in public in Paris, for example, in the Bois de Bologne.

55 [P.52] Kafka, "Reise Lugano—Mailand—Paris—Erlenbach" in *Max Brod, Franz Kafka: Eine Freundschaft*, 1: 183.

56 [P.52] Franz Kafka, *Tagebücher*, 3 vols., ed. Hans-Gerd Koch, Michael Müller, and Malcolm Pasley (Frankfurt am Main, 1994), 1: 42 f.

57 [P.54] Kafka, "Reise Lugano—Mailand—Paris—Erlenbach" in *Max Brod, Franz Kafka: Eine Freundschaft*, 1: 181 f.

58 [P.55] Kafka, *Tagebücher*, 1: 61 f.

59 [P.57] In July 1912, Gaumont's German distributor announces the opening of a short film that bears the same title as Kafka's novel in progress, *Der Verschollene (The Man Who Disappeared)*. The announcement for this film is shown below.
↓

Letzter Bestelltermin
für Programm Nr. **30**
lieferbar am **27. Juli 1912**

No.	Programm Nr. 30	Länge m.	Virage Mk.	Kolorat Mk.
	Dramatisch.			
3869	Der Roman eines Verschollenen	324	25,95	

We possess no more traces of this film today than we do of the "nature shots" of New York, which, almost like an album, mark the stages of Karl Rossman's arrival in the New World. The announcement for this film is shown below.
↓

Oktober 1908.
1. Woche.

2. Serie.

Natur-Aufnahmen.

2426
Telegr.-Adr.: *Fanal.*

New-York.

Länge 155 m.   Preis Mk. 155.—

Titel der einzelnen Bilder.

Statue der Freiheit (von Bartholdi)
Ankunft eines Dampfers im Hafen
Ellis Insel -- Die Station der Auswanderer
Auswanderer an Bord eines Dampfers — Ausschiffung
Broadway — Ansicht des Hauses St. Paul
Einige Wolkenkratzer — Haus der City Investing Co.
Häuser von 50 Etagen im Bau
Brooklyn-Brücke
Die öffentlichen Promenaden im Central-Park

The individual New York "nature shots" listed in the advertisement are the Statue of Liberty (by Bartholdi); the arrival of a steamship in the harbor; Ellis Island—waystation of emigrants; emigrants on board a steamship—disembarking; Broadway—view of St. Paul's Church; some skyscrapers—the City Investing Co. building; fifty-story buildings under construction; the Brooklyn Bridge; and public promenades in Central Park. —TRANS.

60 [P.57] Kafka, *Tagebücher*, 2: 70.

61 [P.57] Kafka, *Tagebücher*, 2: 70.

62 [P.58] In this context, the few published sketches and line drawings by Kafka, elegant and slightly mad, should be read as a literally "expressionist" condensation of cinematic images.

63 [P.58] Letter dated December 17, 1934. In *Theodor W. Adorno / Walter Benjamin: Briefwechsel, 1928–1940*, ed. Henri Lonitz (Frankfurt am Main, 1994), 95.

64 [P.59] Franz Kafka, *Der Verschollene. Roman*, ed. Jost Schillemeit (Frankfurt am Main, 1994).

65 [P.59] Franz Kafka, *Briefe an Felice und andere Korrespondenz aus der Verlobungszeit*, eds. Erich Heller and Jürgen Born (Frankfurt am Main, 1967), 163.

66 [P.61] Kafka, *Tagebücher*, 2: 79.

67 [P.62] Kafka, *Briefe an Felice und andere Korrespondenz aus der Verlobungszeit*, 66 f.

68 [P.62] Kafka, *Tagebücher*, 2: 103.

69 [P.64] Richard Rosenheim, *Die Geschichte der Deutschen Bühnen in Prag, 1883–1918* (History of the German Theaters in Prague, 1883–1918; Prague, 1938), 207, 216.

70 [P.65] *Der Kinematograph* [Düsseldorf], no. 297 (1912).

71 [P.65] At Sedan, a city in northern France, the Germans defeated the French in 1870. –TRANS.

72 [P.67] Kafka uses the slang term "Jargontheater," or "dialect theater," which in this context refers exclusively to the Yiddish dialect. –TRANS.

73 [P.67] Kafka, *Briefe an Felice und andere Korrespondenz aus der Verlobungszeit*, 73.

74 [P.68] Kafka, *Briefe an Felice und andere Korrespondenz aus der Verlobungszeit*, 324.

75 [P.68] Kafka, *Briefe an Felice und andere Korrespondenz aus der Verlobungszeit*, 320.

76 [P.68] Elias Canetti, *Kafka's Other Trial: The Letters to Felice* (New York: 1982), 40.

77 [P.69] Kafka, *Briefe an Felice und andere Korrespondenz aus der Verlobungszeit*, 324 f.

78 [P.70] Kafka, *Briefe an Felice und andere Korrespondenz aus der Verlobungszeit*, 325.

79 [P.70] Alfred Kerr, review in *Vossische Zeitung*, November 6, 1910.

80 [P.71] Franz Kafka, *Briefe, 1902–1924*, ed. Max Brod (Frankfurt am Main, 1958).

81 [P.71] Kafka, *Briefe an Felice und andere Korrespondenz aus der Verlobungszeit*, 325 f.

82 [P.72] Albert Bassermann, "The Actor in the Cinema and on Stage," *Bohemia*, January 30, 1911.

83 [P.73] Kafka, *Briefe an Felice und andere Korrespondenz aus der Verlobungszeit*, 325 f.

84 [P.73] Kafka, *Briefe an Felice und andere Korrespondenz aus der Verlobungszeit*, 279.

85 [P.73] Otto Pick, review of *Reflection* by Franz Kafka, *Bohemia*, January 30, 1911.

86 [P.74] Kafka, *Briefe an Felice und andere Korrespondenz aus der Verlobungszeit*, 326.

87 [P.75] Kafka, *Briefe an Felice und andere Korrespondenz aus der Verlobungszeit*, 326.

88 [P.75] The Bassermann film. —A lot of writer-films await us. *The Other*, by Paul Lindau, has as its subject, as is well known, the problem of a pathological double life. A state prosecutor who becomes a burglar at night, without his two consciousnesses knowing about each other... A fall from a horse has made the lawyer ill. At night, he sneaks into the thieves' den and breaks into his own house with a band of criminals, without remembering even a single step afterward. A theme that is suitable for a novel, perhaps for a play, as well, but certainly not for a film. The novel will treat it with all the epic possibilities for exploiting situations; the play, whose acts can reveal the threads that lead forward and backward, will be able to gain credibility by means of the differences in speech between the prosecutor and the criminal; but the film, which shows a fall from a horse and then, all of a sudden, a human being whose intelligent face is twisted into the mask of a criminal, merely presents the bare facts, without the finer motivations. It does not demonstrate and convince. Besides, Lindau's opus is a very bad film. Verbal statements take the place of events that are important for the eye, the exposition has nothing to do with the actual problem, the film starts too early, and then there is not enough time to expand important episodes of the primary plot. That the state prosecutor was once a harmlessly happy man is something we believe or can rapidly be shown, without wasting a whole act on it. But it was important to show how he slowly recovers physically from the fall and how the dark attack of his second ego assaults him for the first time, how he struggles against it like a bodily affliction and finally succumbs. Instead of motivating the problem of the "Other" with all possible means, a completely arbitrary secondary plot is carried out with great commotion—a servant girl of the prosecutor's secret lover is unjustly suspected of the burglary, is dismissed, and is forced to become a waitress in the very thieves' den that the state prosecutor visits, and must finally convince him of his double life by means of concrete evidence. *The Other* by Lindau is thoughtless in the worst sense, a fiasco of the most terrible sort for the writer-film. Ulrich Rauscher, "Der Bassermann Film, " *Frankfurter Zeitung*, February 6, 1913. Reprinted in *Kein Tag ohne Kino*, 140 f.

89 [P.75] Kafka, *Briefe an Felice und andere Korrespondenz aus der Verlobungszeit*, 338.

90 [P.77] *Uriel Acosta*, a tragedy by Karl Gutzkow.

91 [P.78] Kafka, *Briefe an Felice und andere Korrespondenz aus der Verlobungszeit*, 336.

92 [P.81] In *Le cinéma et l'écho du cinéma réunis*, no. 60, April 18, 1913.

93 [P.81] In fact, there are no diary entries for the period between February 28 and May 2, 1913.

94 [P.81] Kafka, *Briefe an Felice und andere Korrespondenz aus der Verlobungszeit*, 336.

95 [P.82] The full poster—including credits for a libretto by Georg Okonkowski and Julius Freund and music by Jean Gilbert—appears below.

↓

96 [P.84] This postcard shows something happening in an onomatographic sense, as well: Ida, Ottla, Russka, Kafka, and the repeated **K** of the **K**ino-**K**önigin.

97 [P.87] Well-known entertainment center and "red light" district in downtown Berlin. –TRANS.

98 [P.89] In *Prolog vor dem Film: Nachdenken über ein neues Medium* 1909–1914, ed. Jörg Schweinitz (Leipzig, 1992).

99 [P.89] Kafka, *Briefe an Felice und andere Korrespondenz aus der Verlobungszeit,* 367 f.

100 [P.90] Kafka, *Briefe an Felice und andere Korrespondenz aus der Verlobungszeit,* 394.

101 [P.90] Kafka, *Briefe an Felice und andere Korrespondenz aus der Verlobungszeit,* 385.

102 [P.91] Kafka, *Briefe an Felice und andere Korrespondenz aus der Verlobungszeit,* 405.

103 [P.91] Kafka, *Tagebücher,* 2: 179.

104 [P.91] Kafka, *Briefe an Felice und andere Korrespondenz aus der Verlobungszeit,* 416 f.

105 [P.91] Kafka, *Tagebücher,* 2: 179.

106 [P.92] Kafka, *Tagebücher,* 2: 179 ff.

107 [P.92] A still from a newsreel about the Romanov tercentenary is shown below.

↓

108 [P.92] In the morning edition of the Prague Tag-blatt of July 1, one can read the following: **Grand Theater—Bio "Elite."** The drama *Fantômas* combines all those powerful effects that are frequently found in well-made detective novels: the secretiveness of the criminal, his incredible cleverness, his courage and the determination with which he is able to triumph over all dangers and escape, and finally the famous trick with which, after he has already fallen into the hands of his pursuer, he escapes from him again. There is something of the detective novel in the second drama, *Slaves of Gold*, as well. Here, too, the plot revolves around the robbery of a millionaire; but the affair ends in such a way that the criminals are chased away in fear and horror, since the cartons of gold contain live snakes. The Wild West milieu in which these events transpire does whatever else is required to grip the viewers. A splendid nature film and a funny grotesque provide the frame for the two great dramas.

An advertisement for the two films is shown below.

↓

109 [P.93] Kafka, *Tagebücher*, 2: 180 ff.

110 [P.94] Kafka, *Tagebücher*, 2: 180.

111 [P.94] Kafka, *Briefe an Felice und andere Korrespondenz aus der Verlobungszeit*, 418 f.

112 [P.94] Kafka to Felice Bauer, August 1, 1913. In *Briefe, 1913 – Marz 1914*, ed. Hans-Gerd Koch (Frankfurt am Main, 1999).

113 [P.95] Kafka, *Briefe an Felice und andere Korrespondenz aus der Verlobungszeit*, 424 f.

114 [P.96] Local historian Ferruccio Ferroni writes of cinema proprietor Calzoni: **Calzoni, who came from Brescia, was the first to open a cinematograph in Verona in early 1907, next to the former parish church of San Sebastiano. On the façade of the Barbiere across from the Palazzo Bertani, two huge, rather odd-looking globes shone with a reddish electric light. A loud, electrically operated bell called the audience from the Via Capella and the Via Leoni. The explanation for the films was provided by a player piano that did its best, as the occasion required, to combine themes and screenplays with emotional or cheerful scores.** From Ferruccio Ferroni, *Verona di ieri* (Verona, 1934), 163.

115 [P.97] Franz Kafka, *Briefe, 1902–1924*, ed. Max Brod (Frankfurt am Main, 1958), 120.

116 [P.97] Kafka, *Briefe an Felice und andere Korrespondenz aus der Verlobungszeit*, 466.

117 [P.98] Kafka, *Briefe, 1902–1924*, 122.

118 [P.98] Kafka, *Briefe, 1902–1924*, 122.

119 [P.98] Kafka, *Briefe an Felice und andere Korrespondenz aus der Verlobungszeit*, 466.

120 [P.100] Kafka, *Briefe an Felice und andere Korrespondenz aus der Verlobungszeit*, 637.

121 [P.100] Kafka, *Briefe an Felice und andere Korrespondenz aus der Verlobungszeit*, 472.

122 [P.100] In a letter from 1920 to Max Brod that looks back on this period with Felice, Kafka writes, **I am not talking about happy... times of childhood, when the door was still shut behind which the court was in session...**, but later it was so that the body of every other girl tempted me, while that young girl in whom I (therefore?) placed my hopes did not. As long as she withdrew from me (Felice) or as long as we were one (Milena), it was only a threat from afar and not even so very far, but as soon as any little thing happened, it all broke apart. Kafka, *Briefe, 1902–1924*, 317.

123 [P.100] Kafka, *Briefe an Felice und andere Korrespondenz aus der Verlobungszeit*, 472.

124 [P.103] Kafka, *Briefe an Felice und andere Korrespondenz aus der Verlobungszeit*, 467.

125 [P.103] Kafka, *Tagebücher*, 2: 203.

126 [P.104] From *Bohemia*, September 14, 1913: **Grand Theatre Bio "Elite."** An actress, barely out of her baby shoes but with all the artistic qualities of a mature artist, plays the lead role in the three-part comedy *There Are No More Children*. It is the little Suzanne Privat, who already gave evidence of a splendid talent in the great film *Das Kind von Paris* (The Child of Paris). In the second film, Lux, the talented police dog, demonstrates his astonishing training. In the drama *Katastrophe am Dock* (Catastrophe at the Dock), finally, a multifaceted plot unfolds. But the high point of the evening is the four-act comedy *Isidors Hochzeitsreise* (Isidore's Honeymoon), or *Endlich Allein* (Alone at Last), starring the well-known comedians the brothers Herrnfeld as well as the lovely and spirited Hanni Weisse. This grandiose multiple bill lasts three full hours; in spite of this the prices have not been increased.

This advertisement and a photograph of the young actress Suzanne Privat are shown below.
↓

127 [P.104] Kafka, *Tagebücher*, 2: 204.

128 [P.105] In *Masken* 4, no. 8 (November 1913).

129 [P.106] *Roland of Berlin*, July 17, 1913.

130 [P.106] Kafka, *Tagebücher*, 2: 209 ff.

131 [P.107] On June 11 1914, he writes to Grete Bloch, who at Felice's request has served as a go-between since the fall of 1913, **A human being who is entirely asocial as a result of his life circumstances and his nature, in less than stable health, which at the moment is difficult to judge, excluded by his non-Zionist (I admire Zionism and am disgusted by it) and nonbelieving Judaism from every large, supporting society, shattered in his most intimate self, in the most torturous way, by the forced labor of the office, decides to marry, that is, to commit the most social act. This seems not a little for such a human being.**

132 [P.109] From *Prager Tagblatt*, October 21, 1921.

133 [P.111] Both reviews in *Selbstwehr*, October 28, 1921. It is probably this issue dated October 28 that Kafka had sent to his friend and doctor Robert Klopstock with the words, "I am sending you the *Selbstwehr* on Monday, no matter if you hunger for it a little, after you have often disdained it in the past," *Briefe, 1902–1924*, 364. Along with the main feature *Shivat Zion*, Kafka was certainly also interested in the report on the Eleventh Zionist Congress in Carlsbad. The speech that was given at the congress by the agronomist Ruppin concerning improvement of the soil in Palestine had been reprinted in the *Selbstwehr* and read attentively by Kafka.

134 [P.111] *Prager Tagblatt*.

135 [P.112] Franz Kafka, *Briefe an Milena*, ed. Jürgen Born and Michael Müller (Frankfurt am Main, 1983), 288.

136 [P.112] Kafka, *Briefe, 1902–1924*, 400.

137 [P.113] Kafka, *Briefe, 1902–1924*, 337.

138 [P.113] A convincing interpretation of the expression "old new country" is given Martin Bäuml: The reference is to the *Altneuschul* [in German, literally "old new school" –TRANS.], the oldest synagogue in Prague. The name comes from the Hebrew *al-tnai*, which means "on condition that," namely, on condition that this house of prayer (in Hebrew, *bjt hakneset* or meeting house) should not look like a synagogue from the outside. If *altneu* derived from Yiddish, it could stand for *altnaj*, but it is absurd to suppose that the expression comes from German when the inscriptions in the synagogue and adjacent cemetery are in Hebrew. Theodor Herzl, the founder of political Zionism and hence the indirect founder of the state of Israel, who did not know Hebrew, called his famous novel about the Jewish state *Altneuland*, and incidentally, imagined that German would be spoken there. The fact that stones from the Second Temple were said to have been used, which were then supposed to be transported back to Jerusalem, probably has something to do with this identification, which was also adopted by Herzl. In this way it is understandable how *al-tnai* could have been transformed into *Altneu*. Martin Bäuml, letter to the editor, *Frankfurter Allgemeine Zeitung*, January 14, 1983.

139 [P.113] Kafka, *Briefe, 1902–1924*, 385.

140 [P.113] Kafka, *Briefe, 1902–1924*, 392.

141 [P.113] Kafka, *Briefe, 1902–1924*, 463.

142 [P.114] Kafka, *Briefe, 1902–1924*, 364f.

143 [P.114] Franz Kafka, *Briefe an Ottla und die Familie*, eds. Hartmut Binder und Klaus Wagenbach (Frankfurt am Main, 1974), 145f.

144 [P.114] Kafka, *Briefe an Milena*, 319.

145 [P.115] Kafka, *Tagebücher*, 3: 193.

146 [P.115] Kafka, *Tagebücher*, 3: 193.

147 [P.117] Unpublished. From Research Center for German Literature in Prague, Bergische University Wuppertal. Translated from the Czech by Marek Nekula.

Shown here are promotional materials for showings of *The Kid* in Paris (below) and Berlin (right). →

↓

BRIEF FILMOGRAPHY

Films in **boldface** are still in existence.

Le Gendarme altéré [The Thirsty Gendarme; German: *Der Durstige Gendarm*], France (Pathé) 1908, length 100 m.

Le galant da la Garde française [The Galant Guardsman], France (Pathé) 1908, length 175 m.

Den hvide Slavehandels sidste offer [The White Slave Girl; German: Die weisse Sklavin], Denmark (Nordisk) 1911; directed by August Blom; script by Peter Christensen; camera by Axel Graatkjaer; with Clara Wieth (Edith von Felsen), Lauritz Olsen (Engineer Faith), Thora Meinecke (Otto Lagoni), Ingeborg Rasmussen (Frederic Jacobsen), Ella la Cour (Peter Nielsen) et. al.; length 930 m.

Nick Winter et le vol da la Joconde [Nick Winter and the Theft of the Mona Lisa], France (Pathé) n.d., directed by Brusquet, length 170 m.

Une intrigue à la cour de Henri VII [An Intrigue at the Court of Henry VII], France (Pathé) 1913, directed by Morlhoz, with Madeleine Roche, M. Volny, Mlle Massart, M. Etievant, length 225 m.

La Tournée du docteur [The Doctor's Rounds], France (Pathé) 1911, directed by Dupuis, with M. Thali, M. Tréville, Mlle Dermoz, length 225 m.

Pêche au hareng en mer du nord [Fishing for Herrings in the North Sea], France (Pathé) 1911.

Theodor Körner, Germany (Deutsche Mutoskop) 1912, length 1,300 m.

Seltsame Insekten [Strange Insects], Germany 1912, length 175 m.

Der Andere [The Other], Germany 1913, directed by Max Mack, script by Paul Lindau, music by Altmann-Nemo, with Albert Bassermann, Hanni Weisse, Léon Resemann, Emerich Haube, Rely Ridon, Otto Collot, Paul Passarge, C. Lengling, 5 acts, length 1,766 m.

La Broyeuse de coeurs [The Heartbreaker], France (Valetta/Pathé) 1913, length 850 m.

La Leçon du gouffre [The Lesson of the Abyss; Italian: La lezione dell'abisso], France (Pathé) 1913.

Le célèbre bandit Garouge [The Famous Bandit Garouge; Italian: Il celebro bandito Garouge], France (Edison) 1913.

Le Collier vivant—Scènes de la vie de l'Ouest américain [The Living Necklace; German: *Sklaven des Goldes* (Slaves of Gold)], France (Gaumont) 1913, directed by Jean Durand, with Berthe Dagmar, Gaston Modot, Max Dhartigny.

Newsreel on the tercentenary of the Romanov Dynasty [Le Tricentenaire de la dynastie Romanoff], length 185 m.

Katastrofen I Dokken [Catastrophe at the Dock], Denmark (Nordisk) 1913, with Richard Jensen, Jonna Neiiendam, Kai Lind, Gudrun Houlberg, Valdemar Møller, Rasmus Ottesen, Peter S. Andersen, Hakon Ahnfeldt-Rønne, length 950 m.

L'Enfant de Paris [Little Lolotte; German: *Die kleine Lolotte*], France (Gaumont) 1913, directed by Léonce Perret, with Suzanne Privat, length 2,436 m.

Endlich allein, oder Isidors Hochzeitsreise [Alone at Last, or Isidor's Honeymoon], Germany (Vitascope) 1913, directed by Max Mack (based on a play by Anton and Donat Herrnfeld), with Anton Herrnfeld, Donat Herrnfeld, Hanni Weisse, three acts, length 1,060 m.

Nur einen Beamten zum Schwiegersohn [Only a Bureaucrat for a Son-in-Law], Germany (Lux) 1913.

Shivat Zion [Return to Zion], Palestine/Germany (Zionist Commission, Jerusalem, and Central Office of the Jewish National Fund), 1920.

The Kid, USA (Chaplin/First National) 1919, written and directed by Charles Chaplin, with Charles Chaplin, Edna Purviance, Jackie Coogan, Carl Miller, Tom Wilson, length 1,615 m.

ILLUSTRATION CREDITS

The German publisher requests the owners of those rights
that could not be located to identify themselves.

[PP.i,vii,11,12,14,17,24,26,40,79,82,96,125,132,136]
From the private archive of Hanns Zischler.

[PP.ii,iv,vi,69,129] Stiftung Deutsche Kinemathek,
Berlin.

[PP.iii,22]: Kirk Vernedoe and Adam Gopnick, *High
& Low: Modern Art and Popular Culture* (New York:
The Museum of Modern Art, 1990). © Roger-Viol-
let, Paris (P.iii); © Ray Moniz; © Ray Strong (P.22).

[PP.v,128] *Pathé. Premier Empire du Cinéma* (Paris
1994). © Éditions du Centre Pompidou (P.v); © Éditions du Centre Pompidou; © Roger-Viollet, Paris
(P.128).

[PP.viii,42,72] Klaus Wagenbach, *Kafka: Bilder aus
seinem Leben* (Berlin, 1991). © Klaus Wagenbach.

[P.6] Cinémathèque Française.

[PP.8,120] Bernard Chardère, ed., *Les Lumières* (Lausanne, 1985).

[P.29] Fotomuseum München (Fotos Gerhard Ullmann).

[PP.53,72,99,134] Bibliothèque Nationale, Paris.

[PP.40,124] National Museum of Czechoslovakia,
Prague.

[P.50] Francis Lacloche, *Architectures de Cinémas*
(Paris, 1981). © M. Renard, Paris; © Roger-Viollet,
Paris.

[P.56] © Hulton Archive / Corbis.

[P.65] Stadtarchiv Kassel.

[P.66] Theaterarchiv Akademie der Künste, Berlin.

[PP.76,80] Restaurations et tirages de la Cinémathèque Française III, 1988.

[P.93] Jean-Louis Capitaine,ed., *Les premières Feuilles
da la Marguerite. Affiches Gaumont, 1905–1914* (Paris,
1994).

[P.122] *Art & Publicité*, exhibition catalog (Paris,
1990). © Éditions du Centre Pompidou.

[P.128] Lamberto Sanguinetti, *Il Teatro Fossati di
Milano* (Milan, 1972).

INDEX

Page numbers in **boldface** are illustrations.
Outlined notes (⬚#) are illustrations.

INDEX

THE TREES
For we are like tree trunks in the snow.
In appearance they lie sleeky and a little push should be enough to set them rolling.
No, it can't be done, for they are firmly wedded to the ground.
But see, even that is only appearance.

Franz Kafka, *Meditation*

Franz Kafka was a Czech writer who wrote in German and worked for an insurance company. Peter Bil'ak is a Czech typographer who designed Fedra Sans for a German insurance company. Beyond these circumstantial connections, however, the pairing of Kafka and Fedra Sans seems particularly appropriate.

The few texts Kafka published during his lifetime with Kurt Wolff Verlag and others were set in modern-style typefaces—Walbaum was a favorite—as well as in informal sans serifs. In so doing, Kafka consciously broke with the German blackletter tradition, a decision no doubt influenced both by his status as a Czech Jew writing outside the mother country and by his desire to set his work apart from German writing of the era.

Fedra Sans might have suited Kafka's taste for the typographic avant-garde. Its freshly observed letterforms integrate references to fifteenth-century Venetians, eighteenth-century frakturs, and twentieth-century grotesques. Its unique features, including a comprehensive Czech character set and a host of unusual ligatures (the "fk" proved particularly useful), more than suited the needs defined by this book.

DESIGNED BY WINTERHOUSE STUDIO

William Drenttel, Rob Giampietro, and Kevin Smith

Falls Village, Connecticut

SEP   2003

LONDON PUBLIC LIBRARY
WITHDRAWN